I0598918

CUDDLES

CUDDLES

ROBERT SCOTT WILT

ASA PUBLISHING CORPORATION
AN INNOVATIVE OUTSOURCE BOOK PUBLISHING HYBRID

ASA Publishing Corporation
An Accredited Hybrid Publishing House with the BBB
www.asapublishingcorporation.com

1285 N. Telegraph Rd., #376, Monroe, Michigan 48162

Book Title: Cuddles
Date Published: 03.16.2021 / Edition 1 *Trade Paperback*
Book ID: ASAPCID2380808
ISBN: 978-1-946746-66-5
Library of Congress Cataloging-in-Publication Data

This book was published in the United States of America.
Great State of Michigan

Table of Contents

-CUDDLES-

VOLUME 1

CHAPTER 1

This is a story of three friends; Dave, Chris and Gary. Dave is the fun and nice-looking guy. He was a jock in school, went out with the nice looking or popular girls and always looked out for Chris and Gary. Chris isn't a bad looking guy, but he is a smartass or the class clown. He almost always had something to say and most of the time, he didn't think before he talked. Gary is a quiet guy or the nerd of the three. He's into computers or video games and don't have any self-confidence. He was raised by his mom and didn't have a male role model growing up. They lived by each other when they were growing up and they've been friends for as long as they can remember.

They've been there for each other through good and bad times. They've always had each other's backs. As they grew older, they still stuck by each other's side. They were so close that they all three ended up working at a local electronics store when they graduated.

Due to online buying, the store wasn't getting the business that they once had. So, most days were pretty slow and boring. They knew that they needed something different that wasn't a dead-end job. They would always try to think of ways to make extra money. Then one day, Dave and Chris were standing around talking when a female coworker ran up to them crying. Her boyfriend had just broken up with her. She was devastated. As she approached them, Chris put his arms out to try to hug her for comfort. She went right by him like he wasn't even there and ran right into Dave's arms. "Oh, apparently I'm invisible," Chris mumbled As Dave was comforting her, she said, "Thanks, and I wish I could repay you for always being there for me."

All of a sudden, Dave got an idea. He said, "I have a way to make some extra money."

Being the smartass that he is, Chris replies, "Sleeping with Angela's not going to make us any extra money. Well, maybe you can make some extra money."

"No dumbass, we're going to start a business helping needy or heartbroken women. We're going to start a cuddling business."

"What? Excuse me, a cuddling business."

"Yes, if someone is alone, going through bad times or just

needs someone to talk to, we'll be there for them."

After Dave said that, Chris instantly started thinking more dirty or perverted thoughts about what Dave was getting at. Chris said, "Yeah we can."

Dave interrupted him and said, "No, we can't."

"What about?"

Once again, Dave interrupted him and said, "Especially not that."

"How do you know, because you never let me finish?"

"I know what you were going to say, and it's still no. Let's go talk to Gary." Even though Dave wouldn't listen to Chris he decided that he would go along with it. They went to talk to Gary in the computer department because he was the computer nerd and they weren't doing it without him. "We have an idea to make some extra money and we want you to be a part of it." Dave said to Gary, "We're going to start a cuddling business."

Gary asked, "A cuddling what?"

"A cuddling business." Dave replied, "If someone is alone, going through bad times or just needs someone to talk to, we can go and be there for them." Gary was skeptical about it because he wasn't quite the ladies' man and was very shy when it came to women.

"What about this place?" Gary asked, "I mean we've been here for over ten years and I'm almost ready to be promoted to assistant manager."

"Forget this place, look at it," Dave replied, "It's always dead in here and people are buying this stuff online."

"Yeah, this place may not be around much longer." Chris said, "Plus, we can use your computer skills to help with the website." Finally after saying something smart, he said something like his normal smartass self. "Yeah you can sit back, handle the money, the computer stuff while me and Dave are going to get us some honies." Then he tried to high five Dave and he just looked at Chris shaking his head.

Gary knew that they were right and had to figure something else out, so he agreed to go along with it. Gary was nervous about it because he never had a girlfriend and didn't know what to expect.

The next day, Gary went over to Dave and Chris's apartment to discuss what they were going to do. They knew that they couldn't quit their jobs just yet, so they were going to work both jobs until they could establish themselves as business owners. They also wanted to make sure that the cuddling business would work out and get the business to make money. They discussed what the guidelines and rules of the business would be. Dave and Gary knew it had to be professional to be legit. Of course, Chris had different ideas but his ideas didn't fly. Chris was looking at this as a chance to hook up and get laid. They all had to reassure each other that it was going to be cuddling only. This way they couldn't get arrested or shut down for prostitution. This made Gary a little more comfortable because he was a virgin and nervous about it in the first place. They went on talking about their ideas about the business and trying to figure things out. They figured out pricing, how to design the website, and the legal stuff that they were going to need to start the business. Once everything was in place, Gary would design the website while the other two would hang up fliers. They were getting pumped up and excited about what could happen. Even Gary was getting on board with the idea. He was still nervous about it but was getting better. Dave and Chris were just hoping that he could keep his composure when he went out for the first couple of times. They figured that it was just cuddling, but knew that bad things could happen. As they were preparing for anything that could happen, they prepared for the worst. They took Gary to a strip club and made him look at porn to help prepare him to be around women. He was nervous and shy about it but went along with it. The strip club was basically Chris's idea and apparently, he had a lot of ones to get rid of.

Weeks passed and they were finally ready to start their business. Like they agreed they would continue to work at the electronics store as well as the cuddling business. They would get off work at the electronics store and go home to check the website to see if there were any appointments. Most of the time, Gary was checking it from the work computer nervously because he was worried that he'd get caught. He was more embarrassed about it than anything because he didn't want to explain what was going on to anyone.

Many days had passed and there were no messages. They all started thinking that maybe this wasn't such a good idea. They went from being really happy or excited, to being depressed or feeling like they'd failed. Finally, one day while they were standing around at work, that all came to an end. They checked the computer and finally had their first appointment. The message said that she wanted to know if someone was available that evening. The next step was figuring out who got to go. Gary got nervous and instantly started making excuses. "One of you two will have to do this because I got this thing and it's really catchy. I really don't think it's a good idea if I give to someone." The other two knew he was just making up excuses so they blew it off. Dave finally spoke up and said, "Chris should go." He felt that if this failed and he talked Chris into going along with the idea, he'd be selfish to do it. Chris was a little nervous and tried to talk his way out of it but it didn't work. Chris said to Dave, "It was your idea and you should go first."

"I talked you into doing this so if it fails, I'll feel really bad." Dave insisted, "This way you at least have an appointment."

Chris figured that he couldn't talk his way out of it, so he finally agreed to do it. After he got off work, he headed home because he had an appointment to go on.

Chris nervously drove over to the woman's house. When he arrived, he sat in the car for a minute until he got the courage to go to the door. Then he finally got the courage, took a deep breath and walked to the door. Once he got to the door, he rang the doorbell and a beautiful woman answered the door. It was like a slow-motion scene in a movie where her hair blows in the wind while she's biting her lip. Chris then thought, "Wait a minute, this isn't that bad."

Chris was just staring at her while he was daydreaming and she asked, "Can I help you?"

He realized he was daydreaming and said, "Hi, I'm Chris and I'm from Cuddles," which was the name that they came up with for the business.

"Come in, my mom's been waiting for you."

Chris with a stupid look on his face said, "Mom?"

"Yeah, she can't get around very good anymore and since my dad passed away, she just wants to lay in bed. I saw a flyer hanging up so I checked out your website and thought it would be nice for her to have someone to spend a little time with, especially since my dad's passing."

This is not what Chris had planned and he knew he couldn't freak out or lose his composure. Then he thought the sooner he did this, the sooner he gets paid and could leave.

"Well, I'll take you to meet mom."

With a big smile he replied, "I can't wait to meet her." She took him into her mom's bedroom to introduce him to her. Chris was a little bummed that he wasn't going to get to cuddle with the woman's daughter. He expected to be cuddling with nice-looking younger women not older ones.

Chris walked in the bedroom behind the woman's daughter and saw her mom lying down in her bed wearing a night gown. He looked at her daughter and thought, "Really." Then he said to her, "Are you sure you're not a little broken up and need someone to snuggle up with?"

"My husband comforts me when I need it. See you kids later and mom, behave."

As she turned to walk out of the room, Chris grabbed her by her shoulder and asked, "What do you mean by behave?"

"My mom can be a little handsy, blunt and rude at times. Other than that, she's a nice lady." Then she left the room and closed the door.

He approached her and said, "Hi, I'm Chris." Before he could finish what he was going to say, the woman's mom interrupted him. "I don't care who you are, now get over here and start cuddling, what's my daughter paying you for?"

He thought, "What the hell." Now he knew what her daughter was talking about when she told her mom to behave. He knew that he had to do it, so he took off his shoes and climbed into the bed.

Once he got into the bed, she talked about how long it'd been since she'd laid next to anyone, since her husband died. She said to Chris, "Yeah he died right where you're lying, in his sleep." Chris didn't want to hear that; he just wanted to cuddle and leave. She then continued telling him the story about how he died. "We were having sex like they did every night, and then one day after they were done, he fell asleep and never woke up." Chris did not want to hear this but knew he had to be professional. He especially didn't want to hear about them having sex. He thought if he didn't say a word that she would eventually shut up. That didn't work, she continued talking about her and her late husband's sex life. She went into details about the two of them. "He would come in here and kiss me like we were in high school. Then he would take my panties off with his teeth."

Chris knew he had to be nice so he asked her, "How long has it been since your husband passed?" He was thinking by the way she was talking, it'd been a while because he couldn't picture anyone that age doing what she was telling him.

She replied, "It's been three weeks."

"Three weeks? I'm surprised that he lasted that long or that you two didn't pop out a hip or something."

"Oh, we did, hips, shoulders and one time my vagina."

"Ok, I don't need to be hearing about that." Then he mumbled, "Apparently, that thing has more use and miles on it than their car did."

"Did you say vagina?" Chris asked. "You know what, never mind I don't need to know that."

She started telling him about when they first met. "I was on the dance floor at a local bar shaking my stuff. Then he came up and started grinding all over me."

Chris mumbled to himself, "Was that before or after the north won the war?"

"What was that? My hearing isn't like it used to be."

"Nothing, I was just talking to myself." He just laid there with his eyes wide open while he had this old lady spooning him and telling him about her sex life. Chris tried to change the subject but she kept going back to talking about sex with her deceased husband.

Finally, she quit talking about her sex life and started asking Chris about his personal life. She asked, "Do you have a girlfriend or a wife?"

"No."

"Good."

Chris was a little confused about what she meant by good. Then as he was thinking that, she grabbed his butt. Chris squirmed and said, "Ok, I'm just here to cuddle." Then she reached around and rubbed his penis. Chris opened his eyes as wide as he could with a surprised look. He grabbed her hand and pulled it away and said, "Like I said, I'm just here to cuddle."

The old lady replied, "Whatever sissy boy you couldn't handle me anyways, I'd probably give you a heart attack too."

Chris couldn't believe that she just said that, but her daughter did tell her to behave. After the hour was up, Chris got up and put his shoes on and started to walk out of the room. Before he left, he stopped and turned back at the old lady and asked, "Did you shit yourself?"

The old lady replied, "I don't know. Probably, I really can't tell anymore." Chris rolled his eyes, shook his head and walked out of the room.

He walked into the living room where her daughter was sitting to get his money. "Oh, time is up already?" she asked. "I must have lost track of time, hold on I'll be right back with your money." She walked into the kitchen to get his money. As she was walking into the kitchen she said, "I hope that she was good."

Chris replied, "She's a nice lady."

She walked back into the living room and asked, "Are we talking about the same woman?" Then she handed Chris his money and said, "Keep the change." It was only five dollars but he didn't care because he just wanted to leave. He was disgusted and embarrassed about what her mom was saying about her sex life and rubbing her hands on him. No matter what she said he was professional and polite to her.

He said, "Thanks and sorry about your loss."

"It was bound to happen with all the sex that they were having. I couldn't even sleep half the time with all the banging on the walls that was going on in there. My husband and I moved in here to help take care of them and thought about moving out so we could have normal days and nights."

Chris rolled his eyes, shook his head, then left. As he was leaving, he thought to himself, that was a whole different level of crazy that he'd never seen.

On the ride back to his apartment, he was thinking about what to tell Dave and Gary. He didn't want to tell them what had actually happened. He knew that they wouldn't let him live it down and didn't want to have to listen to them because he'd be hearing about it for a long time. He took the long way home so he would have more time to come up with something to tell them. When he got home, Dave and Gary were anxious to hear how it went. "She was beautiful and it went great." "She takes care of her mom because her dad passed away and she needed a break so she messaged us." They continued to ask questions and Chris continued to lie to them. They were trying to see what they had to look forward to, if the business started to pick up.

Dave asked, "Where did you cuddle at?"

He replied, "In her bed."

Gary asked, "Who decided that you were going to cuddle in the bed?"

"She did and I think she was into me." After he said that, Gary was getting a little nervous because he thought it had something to do sexually.

Dave asked, "How do you know that she was into you?"

"Well she asked if I had a girlfriend or was married. Then when I said no, she grabbed by butt."

Gary asked, "What did you do after she grabbed your butt?"

"I told her that I was there to cuddle and that was all."

Gary eventually went home because the three of them had to work in the morning.

A couple of days passed and they finally got another appointment. Chris and Dave were just sitting there watching television after work. They actually got excited because they finally got another appointment. This time it was Dave's turn to go since Chris went the first time. He went to get ready for the appointment. When he was ready, he drove over to the house then went up and knocked on the door. A pretty woman opened the door and Dave told her who he was. "Hi, I'm Dave from Cuddles."

"I'm Kim, come on in." They went and sat down on the couch. "I just moved here not that long ago and don't really know anyone." "I got a promotion at work and didn't have anyone to celebrate with, then I saw one of your flyers so I thought I'd give it a try." There was a bottle of wine sitting on the coffee table.

He thought to himself that he was there to have sex.

Kim asked Dave, "Do you drink and is wine ok?"

Dave said, "Yes I drink, but I'm here to just cuddle and I'm not allowed to have sex."

She assured him that she didn't want to have sex. "I like sex just as much as everyone else, but I don't sleep with just anyone. You're a good-looking guy but I just met you and the wine is just for celebration. If you don't drink or want any wine that's fine, I can get you something else if you would like."

"Wine's fine, there's no better way to celebrate."

The two cuddled with each other on the couch, talked and drank wine. She told him about where she came from and about her job. "I moved here from Michigan and work in advertising. I've been single for quite some time and since I moved, I don't have any friends to be here for me anymore."

"You're a pretty woman and you'll be fine."

"What about you? How did you get into the cuddling business?"

"A coworker's boyfriend broke up with her and she came to me for help. It felt good to be able to help her. Not everyone has someone to go home to, so if they have a bad day, they don't have someone to hold them and help them get through it." "You're telling me," she replied.

"That's sweet of you and a great thing to do for someone." Especially since she was one of those people that didn't have anyone to go home to. They had a nice conversation and she was glad to be able to celebrate with someone. After time was up, she handed him some money and said, "Keep the change."

Dave asked, "Have you ever went out anywhere since you've lived here?"

She replied, "I've been to the grocery store, a few other stores and a few restaurants."

"There's a club called BJs that me and my friends go to on the other side of town, if you ever want to get out of the house."

"I've been to a few bars with some coworkers but not any on the other side of town."

Dave said, "If you ever decide to go there and I'm there, feel free to say hi."

"I don't go out that much but if I ever do, I'll make sure I say hello." Then she walked him to the door, gave him a big hug and said, "Thank you." As he was walking to his car, she told him once again, "Thanks and it was nice meeting you."

"It was nice meeting you too, and congratulations on your promotion." He felt good about what had happened and started getting confidence that this would work. He went back to the apartment and told Chris about his experience.

CHAPTER 2

The next day at work wasn't like most days. It was actually pretty busy. Then Dave noticed an attractive woman looking around the televisions. She seemed kind of lost, so he went over there to see if she needed help. She needed a new television and didn't really know what one she wanted. He continued talking to her and helping her to try to find the right television. She was laughing and having a good time while she shopped for a television.

Chris and Gary noticed them talking and laughing, so they started mocking him. Gary said, "Hi I'm Dave, can I help you?"

Then in a woman's voice Chris said, "Yes can you help me pick out a television?"

Gary responded, "Yes that's my job."

Chris said, "You are such a hero and a kind person to help a poor innocent woman."

Gary added, "Would you like me to carry it out to your car for you?"

Chris replied," Oh that would be so great and you are so strong."

After about twenty minutes, she picked out a television and they proceeded to the cash register so she could pay for it. Then Dave came over to where Chris and Gary were standing. They started messing with him about helping the woman. Chris said, "Oh baby I'm in need of a new television."

Gary added, "Well there's a nice big one right here that you might like."

Chris replied, "I don't know if I can handle that big of a television."

Gary said, "Well I can help you carry it if you would like."

"Are you two done? It was nothing, I was just doing my job," even though Dave did think she was pretty and the other two could tell that he liked her. The three of them finished their shift and decided that they would go out that night for a few drinks.

Later that night, they went to the club for some drinks. They were hanging out around the bar, talking and listing to the music. Then Chris noticed the girl that Dave was helping earlier at the store and she kept looking over at them. "Dave there's the woman from earlier and she keeps looking over here."

Dave asked, "Who?"

"The woman that you helped with the television. Go over there and talk to her."

Dave just kept blowing Chris off because he didn't think she was interested in him. "She's probably just looking around." Dave said, "Why would she be looking over here at me?"

Chris insisted, "Just go talk to her."

He finally decided to go over there and talk to her. He went over there and started talking to her about her television that she bought earlier. "So, how's the new television?"

"Hey there." She said, "Me and my boyfriend broke up and he took one of the televisions when he left. You didn't come over here to talk about televisions, did you?"

"No, by the way I'm Dave."

"Nice to meet you Dave, I'm Heather." They continued talking and laughing while the other two just watched.

"What do you do for a living?"

"I sell houses and you wouldn't happen to be looking to buy a house, would you?"

"Not at the moment but if I was, I definitely would buy one from you."

As Dave was talking to Heather, Chris and Gary started mocking him again like they did in the store. Chris said, "This is exactly how pornos start." Then he mockingly said, "Remember me,

I'm the guy that sold you your television."

Gary responded, "Would you like me to come and hook it up?"

Chris replied in a woman's voice, "Oh yes, then when we're done, we can make love to each other until the sun rises."

Gary added, "We can spank each other all night long."

Chris looked at Gary, shook his head and asked, "What are you, three?"

Gary looked at Chris with an embarrassed look and wondering what he said wrong. Finally, Dave and Heather walked over to where Chris and Gary were hanging around. Dave introduced her to them. "This is Heather." Then he told Heather, "This is Chris and Gary. They were probably over here mocking us when we were over there talking." Chris and Gary both had a nervous look on their faces when Dave said that.

Chris said, "No, we were just over here drinking our drinks and listening to the music.

Gary added, "Yeah, we were just over here drinking, listening and singing because this is our favorite song."

Dave asked, "Whatever, do you guys want to come over here and sit down?" They all decided to go to the table that Heather and her friends were sitting at and hang out over there.

When they walked over to the table, Heather's friends were getting ready to leave. Heather said, "See you guys later and be careful."

Dave said, "It was nice meeting you guys." They told Dave that it was nice meeting him and then they left.

Heather said," Well it looks like it's just us."

Dave replied, "Well it looks like we need a few drinks." Then he stopped a waitress and ordered a round of drinks.

Chris asked Heather, "What do you do for a living?"

Heather answered, "I'm a real estate agent."

Chris looked at Gary and said, "Really? If you know a doctor that can cut an umbilical cord then you can unattach Gary from his mom and sell him a house."

Gary replied, "I'm not attached to my mom, she raised me as a single parent so I stay there to help her out."

Dave said, "Chris has a point, you really should remove your mouth from her nipple."

Gary replied, "My mouth is not on my mom's nipples."

Chris added, "Your mouth is all over those nipples." As he was saying it, he was making the motions of what he was saying.

Heather said, "Well, I think it's a good thing that he helps his mom out."

Gary was done with them messing with him so he tried to change the subject. He said, "Well, you said that these two were going to make a porno."

Dave and Heather looked at Chris in shock.

"No, I didn't, I said this is how pornos start. Think about it, the woman buys a television, a man hooks it up and next thing they're naked in bed or the floor." Then he looked at Gary and said, "Well, you said that they were going to spank each other."

Gary mumbled, "Well, no, but you started it."

"How old are you two?" Dave asked.

Then he looked at Heather and said, "I'm sorry about these two immature idiots."

"It's no big deal." Heather jokingly replied, "Kids will be kids."

Dave said, "Especially these two."

Heather said, "Well it's getting late and I have a house to show in the morning so I'm going to leave."

Dave said, "Yeah Gary has to work in the morning so we probably should leave too. Can I have your number and maybe we can go out sometime?"

Heather answered, "Yeah I would like that." Dave and Heather exchanged numbers then they left to go home.

Gary drove to the club, so when he dropped Chris and Dave off, he decided to come in so they could check the website.

As they were walking in the apartment Chris was saying, "Well that's exactly like a porno and I bet I can find it online right now."

"I don't care, you just don't say that around a woman that

you just met." Dave replied, "I'll be lucky if she calls me after you two idiots."

Chris said, "If not, maybe you can do porn."

Dave replied, "Enough, let's go check the website." After checking it they had two messages. Dave and Chris decided that they would go on the appointments because Gary had to work the next day. He was relieved because since the other two had already had a turn, he was worried that he would have to go.

The next day, Dave and Chris figured out who was going to which appointment. Dave was the first to have to leave for his appointment. He arrived at the woman's house and knocked on the door. A woman answered the door and Dave said, "Hi, I'm Dave from Cuddles."

"Come on in and have a seat." She said, "By the way I'm Cindy." They walked over and sat on the couch. "Thanks for coming, me and my girlfriend broke up so I figured that I could use the company."

Dave sat down by her on the couch, cuddled with her and talked to her about her situation. He asked, "So what happened?"

It ended up being a real stupid reason that they broke up. "Well she went out and then she ended up falling asleep on the couch."

"What's wrong with that? A lot of people fall asleep on the couch."

"She's never done that before and I think she might be cheating on me."

"Did you talk to her about it?"

"Yes."

"What did she say?"

"She said that she was watching television and fell asleep."

"You're probably blowing this out of proportion because I fall asleep watching television on the couch all the time. How long have you guys been going out?"

"Not that long."

"I think you over reacted. You should call her and work things out."

She realized that Dave was probably right and said, "You're probably right and I'll call her later."

Dave calmed Cindy down and they continued talking.

"How did you get into the cuddling business?"

"I helped out a coworker whose boyfriend broke up with her and it felt good, so here I am."

"Do you feel good now because you helped me out?"

Dave asked, "Do you feel good?"

She replied with a smile, "A little."

Dave smiled and said, "I guess it's a little for me too."

As they were talking, her ex-girlfriend just happened to walk in to get something that she left there. She didn't know what was going on and started freaking out because of those two sitting on the couch together. She thought that she was cheating on her and accusing her of cheating. She yelled, "OH YOU ACCUSE ME OF CHEATING, THEN I COME OVER HERE AND CATCH YOU WITH A STRANGE MAN!"

"This is Dave from Cuddles." Cindy explained, "I was depressed that me and you broke up so I messaged him to come over because I could use the company. He made me realize that I was wrong and that I should call you to work things out, plus he's not really even that good looking."

Dave sat there after she said that with a confused look on his face.

Cindy said, "I love you and don't want to fight anymore." Then she gave her a hug and a kiss on her cheek.

"I love you too and don't want to fight anymore either."

Then they both sat down on the couch, cuddled with Dave and the three of them talked. Cindy said, "Dave, this is Nikki; and Nikki, this is Dave."

Dave and Nikki said, "It's nice you meet you."

While they were sitting there talking, Dave asked Cindy, "Did you really mean it when you said that I wasn't good looking?"

She replied, "You're alright but you're not my type."

Then she looked at Nikki and said, "She's my type."

Nikki said, "If I was into dudes, I'd do you."

Dave just sat there with another confused look and shrugged his shoulders. The three of them sat there talking until the time was up. Nikki asked Dave, “So what is Cuddles?”

“It’s a cuddling business.”

“Is it a cuddling business or a way to go have sex with women?”

“We don’t have sex. It’s for women that don’t have anyone and could use some company.”

Cindy said, “Yeah like me.”

Dave jokingly replied, “Yeah like her. I had a woman the other day that got a promotion at work and no one to celebrate it with. I went and cuddled with her so that she had someone to celebrate with.”

“That’s actually a good thing to do for someone.” Nikki replied, “Well, look what you did for us.”

Time was up and Dave said, “I’d love to stay and chat but I think that you two have some making up to do.”

“Yeah I think we do.” Then Cindy said, “I’ll be right back with your money.” Then she went to get Dave’s money so she could pay him. After she came back and paid him, they said, “Thanks.”

“No problem,” Dave replied.

Then Cindy and Nikki gave him a hug then walked him to the door so he could leave.

As Dave was on his way home Chris was on his way to his

appointment. He was just hoping that it goes better than the first time. When he got to the house, he went up and knocked on the door. He heard a woman yell, “I’LL BE THERE IN A SECOND.”

He started looking around and saw a woman walking her dog on the sidewalk. He waved and said, “Good afternoon” to the woman. Then he heard the door open, and turned around to see someone that looked like a transgender man or a real ugly woman standing there. He did a double-take at the person, then he said, “Is this a joke?”

“No.”

“You’re a guy.”

“No, I’m not.”

“Yes, you are.” “You have hairs growing out of your chin.”

“A lot of women have hairs on their chin.”

Chris mumbled, “Yeah, you’re right. You have a deep voice.”

“A lot of women have deep voices.”

Once again Chris agreed.

“Even if I was a man, it doesn’t say anything on your website about no men.”

Chris whispered to himself, “Shit, Gary needs to change that.” Then said, “So you are one hundred percent sure that you’re not a man?”

“Yes, would you like me to show you?”

“Oh, hell no, definitely not.” Chris decided to go along with it because she had a point and just maybe she's really a woman. If she is a woman, she was a very ugly one but still it was his job to cuddle with her.

He went into the house and asked, "What was the reason that you messaged me?" Chris figured it was because she was so ugly and couldn't get anybody.

"I just wanted to try it."

"Really you wanted to try it?"

"I know it's probably shocking to you but I'm single and get a little lonely."

"What's going to be shocking is me going over to the wall socket and sticking my finger in it."

The woman laughed and said, "You're silly. Do you do this in the bedroom or living room?"

Chris was frustrated and said, "Anywhere, let's just get this done."

"Let's go in the bedroom because it's more comfortable."

"Remember this is just cuddling and there's no sex."

"That's fine but that's your loss."

"My loss?"

"Yes, because you could've had all of this." Then she pointed at her body.

"The only thing I'm about to lose is my lunch."

"I would've rocked your world."

After she said that Chris started to think about what she meant and said, "Oh here it comes." Then he started to gag.

"Now you're just being silly, are we going to do this or not?"

Chris didn't want to but had no choice because it was his job and he didn't want to let the other guys down.

The woman got into her bed and patted on it for Chris to lie down next to her.

Chris took off his shoes, then got into the bed next to her. He laid there with a mad look on his face and hoped that this would go by fast.

The woman asked, "I bet a cute guy like you gets all the women wanting to cuddle with you?"

Chris didn't want to talk to the woman but had to be nice and just wanted this to be over. This was like a bad dream for him. "Well, the business just started and you're my second appointment."

"Lucky you because you just hit the jackpot."

"Jackpot?"

"Cuddling with me because I know I'm way better looking than the other woman."

Chris mumbled to himself, "I doubt you're better looking than anybody."

"What did you say?"

"I just said that she was a nice lady." Chris thought to himself that he would rather be cuddling with the old woman and listening to her talk about sex. He really didn't want to listen to this woman talk about how lucky he is to be cuddling with her. He just wanted this nightmare to end. He decided he was just going to lie there until his time was up.

That didn't work, the woman kept talking. "Do you even want to know my name?"

Chris really didn't care but asked, "Sure, what is your name?"

"I'm Lucy, and you are?"

"I'm Chris."

"Nice to meet you Chris, aren't you supposed to tell me this when you first get here so I know that you're not a rapist?"

"Trust me, I don't think anyone is going to try to rape you."

"They better not because I know karate."

Chris mumbled, "Your looks will hit them hard enough."

Lucy asked, "Did I ever tell you that I'm a really good singer?"

"No, you didn't."

"Would you like me to sing for you?"

"Please don't."

Then Lucy started singing to Chris. Chris yelled, "OK THAT'S GOOD. I just have a headache."

Lucy said, "I'm also a really good dancer." Then Lucy started trying to dance while she was cuddling with Chris. Chris just laid there and let Lucy do what she was going to do. Lucy quit doing it after a few seconds. Lucy said, "Maybe one day we can go sing karaoke and go dancing."

"No that's definitely not going to happen."

"I get it, you're just shy around beautiful women."

"Yes, I'm shy so let's just lay here and enjoy the moment." He wanted her to shut up so he would try about anything at this time. Lucy kept rattling on until the time was up.

When the time was up, Chris said, "Ok it's time, and I have stuff to do." He went to get out of bed and she wouldn't let him up.

"What would it cost me to keep you here all night?"

"Excuse me?"

"We are having so much fun, why let it end?"

"As much fun as we are having, I don't have my toothbrush and my breath is going to start stinking real soon."

"You can use mine. I have really clean teeth and don't have gingivitis."

"I just remembered that I have another appointment tonight. As a matter of fact, I'm late right now." Finally, Chris got his money and started to leave. Then he stopped to ask Lucy a question. He knew he was going to regret it, but did it anyways. "So how was it?"

"Ok."

"Just ok," Chris said in a sarcastic way. "But you want me to stay all night." Chris rolled his eyes, shook his head and left.

As Chris was walking to his car Lucy yelled out the door, "MAYBE ONE DAY WE CAN GO OUT TO DINNER?"

Chris just hurried up to his car and acted like he didn't hear anything. He just hoped that no one had seen him leaving the house. Once again, he knew he couldn't tell Dave and Gary about what had happened. He figured that he would tell them it was another pretty woman and it went great.

When Chris got to the apartment, Dave was getting ready to walk out the door because he had a date with Heather. Dave asked, "How did it go?"

"It went good."

Dave said, "Cool." Then he continued on his way out the door. While Dave was on his way to pick up Heather, he knew that he couldn't tell her about the cuddling business yet. When he got there, she wasn't quite ready, so he waited for her in the living room until she was ready. He didn't wait too long because she was almost done.

On the way to the restaurant, Heather was telling Dave about her ex-boyfriend. "He is a really jealous person and won't leave me alone. He's not violent, he's just annoying. I just wanted to let you know just in case things work out between us and we continue to see each other."

Dave didn't know what to think about what Heather said,

but he liked Heather so he didn't care. He replied, "It's no big deal."

When they got to the restaurant they went in and sat down. Heather asked, "Have you ever eaten here before?"

"Yeah, A few times."

Heather said, I really like the food here."

Dave replied, "Yeah, it's not bad." The waitress came over and took their drink order, then went to get them. After she came back with their drinks, she took their food order. The food and conversation were really good. Dave thought to himself that he really liked her and hoped that they can continue to see each other. Dave ended up taking her home and walking her up to her door. He said, "I had a really good time, and would like to see you again."

"I had a really good time too and definitely would like to see you again."

Before he left, she gave him a hug, kiss on the cheek and said, "Thanks again for dinner." Dave stood there for a second surprised, then he walked to his car so he could head home. As he was leaving, her ex-boyfriend was parked down the road watching what was going on.

The next day, Chris and Dave had to work. While they were at work a message came through that said, "I'm freaking out, I just want to die." She wanted someone right now.

Gary was the only one around that could go. He'd always gotten out of going, and never had to do it so he didn't know what to do. He did what he thought he had to and told her that he'd be over. He hurried up and got ready so that he could head over to her house. When he was ready, he left to go over there. When he got there, he walked up to the door and rang the doorbell. A younger looking girl answered the door. Gary was a little confused and didn't know what to do. He asked, "Is your mom home?"

"No."

"I'm Gary from Cuddles and someone left a message to come over here."

"I messaged you."

"Are you eighteen?"

"Yes." He felt a little relieved but still nervous because he didn't know if she was lying to him about her age. She said, "Come in." He was skeptical about it but he went in anyways to see what was going on.

She walked over to the couch and said, "Come on over and have a seat."

Gary walked over to the couch and sat down next to her. He sat there stiff as a board and barely put his arm around her. There was probably a foot between them because he was scared and nervous. Gary didn't even know if this was cuddling or not because he'd never done it before. She looked at him and scooted over closer to him. Gary took a deep breath and stared straight ahead. They both seemed a little nervous. After a few minutes Gary finally asked,

"What did you want?"

"I want to die because I wasn't accepted into the college that I really want to go to. I worked really hard to get in there, I couldn't work any harder. Now I don't know what I'm going to do."

Gary really didn't know what to say because he had no experience dealing with women and their emotions, especially teenagers. He asked, "Did you talk to her mom or dad about this?"

"My mom's divorced, works two jobs to take care of the house, and I haven't seen my dad in years. I really don't want to bug my mom about this because she's got enough going on already."

Then Gary asked, "What about any friends or a boyfriend?"

"I don't have many friends or a boyfriend because I'm focusing on my education. I saw the web site and could use the company so I messaged you. I'm sorry, I'm sure you don't want to deal with this. You probably have your own problems."

"No, you're not bugging me. The business was designed to help women with their problems or women that just want company. Actually, I kind of understand what you're going through."

The girl looked at him with a puzzled look.

"My mom was a single parent, I worked really hard in school, I don't have many friends and I'm a virgin too."

"Wait, you're a virgin? I just said that I didn't have many friends or a boyfriend but I'm not even a virgin."

Now Gary was really confused and didn't know what to say.

"I didn't say I was a virgin."

"Um, yes you did."

Gary tried to talk his way out of this, "You must have misunderstood me, I never said that."

"No, you specifically said bla bla bla, I'm a virgin."

Gary nervously said, "Ok, alright, anyways."

"You know that there's websites for that." She said, "As a matter of fact, instead of a cuddling business, you could've started a . . ."

As she was saying that Gary interrupted her. "OK, I GET IT!" he exclaimed. "What college did you say that you wanted to go to and why didn't you get accepted?" He asked that so that he could change the subject about him being a virgin.

She told him what college she wanted to go to and the reason that she didn't get accepted.

"There are other really good schools out there where you can still get a really good education." "You can go to another school for a year or so, then maybe you can finish up at the school that you originally wanted to go to. Your life's not over, it's just beginning." He was still very nervous because he still wasn't quite sure of her age and worried that her mom would come home. Then when the time was up, the girl stood up and said, I'll be right back." He didn't know what she was going to do and didn't want to get caught in the house so when she walked out of the room, he got up left. He was so nervous and just wanted to get out of there that he didn't even think about getting paid. He decided that he wouldn't even bring this up to the other two and hoped that they didn't see the message. He was going to delete it as soon as he got home.

The next day at work, Gary was being quiet and blowing off the other two. He was still nervous about what had happened the night before. He was looking around all day thinking that the police would come and arrest him because the girl was a minor. Dave and Chris didn't think anything of it because Gary was normally a quiet guy that stays to himself. They also never knew about what had happened the night before because Gary deleted the message before they could see it. The three of them were talking about the business. Dave said, "It would be nice if things would pick up." Chris and Gary both really didn't care but they didn't want to disappoint Dave because this was his idea.

Chris played it off and replied, "It's too bad that it's not going like we had hoped."

Dave said to Chris, "Especially for you, seeing how you've had a couple of hotties."

"What? Chris asked, "Who are you talking about?"

"The two pretty women that you cuddled with."

Chris remembered that he told them that he cuddled with two pretty women. "Oh them. I was still thinking about the business picking up and didn't really hear what you said."

Dave said to Gary, "Maybe one day you'll get your turn."

Gary wasn't really paying attention to what Dave said. Then he nervously said, "Why, what did she say?"

Dave replied, "What did who say?"

Gary said, "No one, it's nothing."

Dave and Chris just looked at him with confused looks. They continued helping customers and waiting for the day to get over. When Gary got a little down time, he would look to see if there were any messages. After looking at the website a few times, he looked it up, rolled his eyes and let out a deep breath. They had two messages and Gary knew there was a chance that he would have to go to one of them. Especially since the other two had been going on appointments and they didn't know that Gary went on one. He went to tell Dave and Chris about the messages so they could figure out who was going to go. Dave was going out with Heather after work so he said, "I'm going out with Heather so you two will have to go." They both agreed, even though they really didn't want to do it. This was exactly what Gary didn't want to hear.

CHAPTER 3

Heather had to show a house that night so she met up with Dave at an ice cream shop. He really liked her, so he didn't care where they met or what they did. They talked, had ice cream, and had another great time with each other. "I haven't had that much fun with a guy in a long time." Heather said, "My ex-boyfriend was a jealous person and he always complained about everything."

"You don't have to worry about anything with me because I'm not a jealous person and I'm probably the funniest guy you'll ever meet."

"Funniest, huh?" She said with a smile, "Is that even a word?"

"I never said I was the smartest."

Heather replied, "Well, I hope so." When they got done

eating their ice cream they went for a little walk. This way, they could waste time until Heather had to go to her appointment. They walked in the park and watched the ducks in the river. While they were walking, Heather grabbed Dave's hand. Dave was surprised that she did that. He wanted to grab her hand but didn't really know how she felt and didn't want to ruin anything. When they were walking back to the ice cream shop, her ex-boyfriend Jason pulled up in his car. Heather walked up to the car and started talking to him. Dave felt very uncomfortable. She talked to him for about a minute then walked back to Dave. She grabbed his arm and pulled him with her. Jason flipped Dave off and drove away. As they were walking away Heather said, "I'm sorry about that, that's my ex-boyfriend Jason."

"Don't worry about it, it's no big deal. Especially after what you told me about him." When they got back to their cars, Dave gave her a hug and she kissed him on his cheek. Once again Dave was surprised and just looked at her for a second. Dave said, "Good luck and be careful."

"Thanks, and you be careful too."

Dave said, "Whenever you get some time tonight, call or text me."

"I will when I get done with my appointment." Then Heather got in her car and started to drive off. As Dave was walking to his car Heather stopped, rolled down her window and said with a smile, "Why would I not text or call the funniest guy that I'll ever meet?"

Dave just looked at her with a smile while she rolled up her window and drove off. Dave got into his car and went home.

Chris and Gary went home after work to get ready for their appointments. Gary's appointment was earlier than Chris' so he had to hurry up and get ready. Once he got ready, he left to go to the woman's house. When he got to the address, there was a biker gang hanging out in the front yard. He didn't know if he should go up to the house or not. He was scared because he didn't know if any of them were the woman's boyfriend or husband. He decided to go up to the house because if she was with someone then she wouldn't have messaged them. Gary forgot what the woman's name was so he pulled out the paper with the address and her name on it. He nervously asked, "Is Lisa home?" One of the guys spoke up and said, "My sister's in the house." Gary went up and knocked on the door. After seeing the biker gang, he wasn't expecting too much of Lisa. Gary was scared because he figured that Lisa would be a scary biker chick.

As Gary was walking up to the door, Lisa's brother yelled, "LISA YOU HAVE COMPANY!" After he yelled, Gary didn't know if he should knock on the door or not. He decided that he would still knock on the door. Anyways. When Lisa came to the door, Gary was surprised. She was not what he expected. She was a short, pretty, and innocent-looking woman. He thought she was really pretty and nervously told her who he was. "Hi, I'm Gary."

"Are you from Cuddles?"

He looked nervously looked around and quietly replied, "Yes."

"Come on in and have a seat." Then they walked over and sat down on the couch. "I messaged you because my parents recently passed away, my boyfriend broke up with me and I really could use some company or someone to talk to."

"Why don't you just talk to your brother?"

"Yeah, he's not the nurturing type."

"I can see that, but he seems really nice."

Gary was nervous because he didn't want her brother to walk in and see them sitting together. He knew that he had to do it, so he sat on the couch with his arm around her. He liked her and got a little excited down in his man land but hid it as best as he could. They watched television and talked about the things bothering her. "My parents got into a car accident and passed away from their injuries, then a few days after the funeral, my boyfriend broke up with me. Other than my brother, I lost everyone that I loved within weeks."

Gary really didn't have experience with this type of stuff so he didn't know what to say. "I'm sorry about your parents and your boyfriend breaking up with you. Especially at a time when you were hurting and needed him the most. I know this is none of my business, but did your boyfriend tell you why he broke up with you?"

"He gave me a lame excuse, but I think he was cheating on me anyways. He tried coming back and talking to me but my brother had a little talk with him. Let's just say that he will never come around me again. My brother is very protective of me and got more protective after our parents passed." Gary was already nervous, but after she said that he got really scared. Lisa could tell that Gary was nervous or scared so she said, "You got nothing to worry about, I told him that I was going to message you guys."

"And he didn't care?"

"Oh hell no, he'd rather me spill my guts to a stranger than him have to listen to me. Don't get me wrong, we talk about stuff but it usually ends up with him telling me to toughen up buttercup."

"That's probably his way of telling you that he loves you."

"Yeah it is, but he'll never admit it. So how did you get into the cuddling business?"

"Well, my friends and I work at the electronics store and one day we decided that we would start a cuddling business. That's pretty much it."

"Don't take this wrong, but you don't seem like the cuddling type."

"What does that mean?"

"You seem like the nice quiet type, not the tell me about your problems type."

"You're right, but Dave and Chris wanted to do it so I'm

doing it for them."

"I know I'm right; I've been talking to you for almost an hour. Don't do it for them, do it for yourself."

"What do you mean?"

"Do you have a girlfriend?"

"No."

"Of course not, you're too nice, quiet and shy. Now when you go to a woman's house to cuddle with her, you're going to snuggle, talk and that will help your shyness." Gary thought that she had a point but he didn't think it would be that easy. They sat there and talked for a little over an hour and Gary had to leave. Lisa went to get money to pay him so he could go. "Thanks for being a gentleman and letting me tell you my problems."

"No problem." Then he held out his hand for her to shake it. Lisa was confused but she shook his hand anyways. Lisa walked Gary to the door so he could leave. After he left, he went to Dave and Chris' apartment to tell Dave about his appointment.

While Gary was on his way to the apartment, Chris arrived at his appointment. He walked up and knocked on the door. A plus size woman with a chicken leg in her hand and barbeque sauce all over her face answered the door. Chris once again knew that this wasn't going to go well. "Hi, I'm Chris from Cuddles."

The woman said, "Come on in, I've been waiting for you. Where do you want to do this?"

He really didn't want to do it at all but knew that had to. "It's up to you, but you might want to go wash up a little." Then he said while pointing at his face, "You have some barbeque sauce on your face." The woman just wiped it with her hand. She decided that she wanted to go into the bedroom so she started walking in there. Chris followed her into the bedroom and was still telling her about the barbeque sauce on her face. Then he looked up in the air like he was talking to the heavens and said, "Whatever I did to make you mad, I'm sorry."

Once they walked into the bedroom, the woman started to take her clothes off. Chris asked, "Excuse me, what are you doing?"

"You can't have sex with your clothes on, silly."

"Sex? Oh no, I'm just here to cuddle, I can't have sex with you because the company doesn't allow it. Do you still want to do this? It's fine if you don't want to because if I go to a restaurant and think that I'm getting a steak but they bring me chicken, I'm going to send it back." He was hoping that she would say no and he could just leave.

She said, "There's nothing wrong with chicken, I like chicken."

"I like chicken too, but I'm expecting a steak and steak is better than chicken."

Then she said, "Why not just eat both, the chicken and the steak?"

Chris finally gave up because he realized that he wasn't going to get anywhere with this woman.

She said, "So cuddling actually means cuddling?"

"Yes, cuddling means cuddling. What did you think it meant?" Then he realized where she got the idea about having sex and said, "Oh no, it definitely means cuddling."

Sarcastically she said, "Since you're here, we might as well just cuddle."

She handed him his money and then laid down in her bed. She motioned for Chris to lie on the bed next to her. Chris said, "You still have barbeque sauce on your face and hands."

The woman asked, "Do you like barbeque sauce?"

Chris said, "Yes."

"Then it won't be a problem."

Chris replied, "I like it on chicken, ribs, or pork chops, but not really on someone's body."

She just smiled then said, "Quit playing and get over here. If we were having sex then it wouldn't be a problem because you could just lick it off."

"Excuse me, I just threw up a little in my mouth. I honestly don't think I can ever eat barbeque sauce again. As a matter of fact, when I get home, I'm throwing the barbeque sauce out, it's going right in the garbage." Then he took a deep breath, rolled his eyes, took off his shoes and got in the bed next to her. When he laid down in the bed, she started to spoon with him. She ended up falling asleep on him, then she started drooling over him. He was all sticky from the barbeque sauce on her hands and face, now he had drool all over him. He even had a chicken bone poking him in his back. He felt nasty and just wanted to go home and shower. He already had his money so when his time was up, he figured he could just leave. This way he didn't have to wake her up. He was just happy that she fell asleep and he didn't have to talk to her. When his time was up, Chris went to get up out of the bed but she was laying on him so that he couldn't get her off him. He ended up falling asleep after trying many times to get out of the bed.

About an hour later she woke up and told him to wake his ass up. "What the hell are you doing? I'm didn't pay you to sleep and don't think I'm paying you anymore money." He shockingly woke up with a confused look on his face and put his shoes on then left.

When he got home, Dave and Gary were sitting around watching television. He went straight to the bathroom, got in the shower, and never said a word. This was weird because he never did that before. Dave and Gary went to the bathroom door to see what happened. They started talking to him through the door. Dave asked, "Is there something wrong?"

Chris hysterically started telling them that he'd been lying about his appointments. He said, "I cuddled with a dinosaur. I cuddled with a transformer or real ugly woman, but I'm pretty sure was a man. Then tonight, I got drooled on, I'm all sticky from barbeque sauce and had a chicken bone sticking in my back. Oh, by the way, I'm throwing out the barbeque sauce and we're never buying it again."

Gary and Dave looked at each other with confused looks on their faces. Chris was making no sense. Then Gary said to Dave, "Transformer?"

"I think he means transgender."

"Oh, what's a transgender?"

"I'll tell you later."

Then Dave and Gary went into the living room, sat down and watched tv. When Chris got out of the bathroom, he walked into the living room, the other two started laughing. Chris said, "Think it's funny, huh?"

Dave said, "You cuddled with a man?"

"First of all, it was either a man, or real ugly woman, because I couldn't really tell. Second, you can't prove anything," Chris said. Then he turned around and started to leave.

Dave asked Chris, "Was that a sucker stuck in your hair?"

Chris stopped, shook his head, and said, "Yes, it was a sucker." Then Chris stormed out of the living room and went into his bedroom.

Dave and Gary started laughing again and hi-fived.

After a little while Chris came back out to the living room.

Then he said to Dave and Gary, “Come on, I know you’re not done.” Then Chris sarcastically said, “Chris cuddled with a man.”

Dave asked, “What’s going on? You cuddled with a dinosaur, a man and barbeque sauce?”

“How did you cuddle with a dinosaur?” Gary asked, “They’re extinct, there’s no such thing as dinosaurs.”

“It was an old woman, but I think she used to have a pet dinosaur and she killed her husband by having sex with him.”

Dave asked, “She had sex with her husband and killed him?”

“According to her, and her daughter, they were having sex like rabbits. Then one day after having sex, her husband didn’t wake up the next morning.”

Then Dave asked, “What’s up with the transgender man?”

“Like I said, it might have been a real ugly woman.” Then he said to Gary, “Oh yeah by the way, you might want to put women only on the website.”

“Explain the barbeque sauce.” Dave said, “Did a woman put barbeque sauce all over her body and want you to lick it off?”

“Trust me, she could’ve put whip cream all over her body and I still wouldn’t lick it off. This woman came to the door holding a chicken leg and barbeque sauce all over. Then when we were cuddling, she fell asleep on me, then she started to drool all over me, and I couldn’t get her off me.”

Dave replied, “That sounds like you were in an old, hard and sticky situation." Then Dave and Gary hi-fived each other while they laughed.

Chris shook his head and said, "I knew that I should never have come back out here." Then he went back into his room.

The next day, Dave and Gary kept messing with Chris at work. They kept making jokes about his appointments. They would say things about having barbeque chicken for lunch or going dress shopping after work. Chris got a little annoyed about those two teasing him, but knew he had it coming once he told them what had happened. "I'm never telling you guys anything ever again." Then he stormed off to help a customer and to get away from those two.

Dave and Gary started laughing then they hi-fived each other. They had no appointments set up for the night or any time for the near future. Gary checked the website periodically throughout the day. Finally, one of the times that he checked it, he closed his eyes and shook his head. There were a lot of messages: some were for that night, and some weren't. He knew that he wasn't getting out of it this time. He walked over to Dave and told him about the messages. Then him and Dave walked over to tell Chris. After work Dave and Chris headed to their apartment while Gary went to his house so they could get ready for their appointments. Then Gary would meet them at their apartment so they could figure out the appointments.

They had four appointments that night so Dave offered to

take two. He felt it was the right thing to do since he'd been spending time with Heather. He also knew that Gary really wasn't into the business and Chris had some bad experiences. Gary wrote down the addresses and handed them out so they could leave. After he handed them out, they started walking towards the door. Chris stopped then he turned around and took the paper out of Gary's hand. Then he handed the paper he had to Gary. Chris took a step towards the door again and stopped. He turned around and looked at Dave. He took one of the papers out of Dave's hand and handed Dave the paper he had. "Not this time. This time one of you can listen to old lady sex stories, cuddle with a man or get all sticky and slobbered on." Then he turned around and walked out the door. The other two just looked at each other and shrugged their shoulders. Then they walked out to go to their appointments.

Chris arrived at his appointment then went up and knocked on the door. He thought that there's no way that this could be as bad as before. Then he heard a voice yell, "COMING!" Then it sounded like two people arguing. A polite, innocent looking woman came to the door and let him in. The woman said, "You must be from Cuddles?"

"Yeah, I'm Chris. Is this a bad time?"

"No, I'm sorry about all the yelling, it isn't polite to fight when company's coming over."

"It's fine, I can always come back another time." He was just wondering whom she was fighting with because there was no one else in the room. He thought maybe the other person just went into the bedroom or something. He also felt kind of weird because he didn't know if it was a boyfriend or husband and didn't want to get into a fight or anything.

The woman politely asked, "Would you like to sit down, and would you like something to drink?"

"No thanks, I'm fine." Then he sat down on the couch and the woman walked away. Chris was confused about what was going on and didn't know if he should be there or not. He thought maybe she was going to talk to the other person that she was arguing with.

The woman walked back into the living room and sat down on the couch. They talked about how their day was going and watched television. Chris thought this isn't so bad. It was definitely a lot better than the other times. All of a sudden, the woman leaned forward, looked over at the other side of Chris and started yelling at somebody or something. "CAN'T THIS WAIT TILL WHEN OUR COMPANY LEAVES?" Chris sat there with a confused look and his eyes wide open. He looked back and forth to try to figure out what was going on. She was just sitting there yelling at nobody. "WE'VE ALREADY DISCUSSED THAT!"

Chris didn't know what to do. He knew that this woman was obviously crazy and didn't know what she was capable of. He thought that there was only one thing to do. He yelled, "LADIES OR

LADY AND GENTLEMAN!" He didn't know who or what she was yelling at. He figured that he had to get her to stop arguing so he could get out of there. He decided he was going to mediate the argument. He ended up getting involved in the conversation and calmed the woman down. "I don't know what's going on here, but you two need to knock it off. You two love each other, I think." It ended up calming her down, and Chris was a little bit relieved.

She said, "We do love each other and need to quit fighting like that."

"You two definitely need to quit fighting. We're here to have a good time, cuddle and relax."

The woman asked, "Well, you've been listening to everything, am I wrong?"

"Excuse me?" He didn't know what to say because he had no idea what was going on.

"I've done everything I can possibly do, I just want to know if I'm wrong?"

Still Chris had no idea what she's talking about so he said, "Well, it's not about who was wrong, it's about how you're going to move on from this. You didn't do everything you could possibly do, there's so much more you can do, I think." Then he looked at the invisible person and said, "Don't think that you're exactly innocent, it takes two of you and there's a lot more you can do too."

The woman leaned forward and said, "That's exactly what

I've been trying to tell you."

Chris said, "Hold on, we're all good so let's not start arguing again."

The woman replied, "You're right."

Chris said, "All this arguing made me thirsty and I could use that drink."

"I could use one too." Then she looked over at the invisible person or thing she was arguing with and said, "Are you sure, I can get it?" After about five minutes the woman said, "Thanks." Then she acted like she picked up a glass and started drinking it."

By this time, Chris knew that this woman was completely nuts. The woman asked, "Don't you like your drink?"

"No, it's fine." Then he acted like he picked up his drink and drank it. Then he said, "That's good."

The woman said, "You didn't even drink it, the glass is still on the table."

Now Chris didn't know what to do, because he didn't know where his drink was supposed to be. He said, "I know, I'm just playing with you." He slowly started moving his had along the table hoping that the woman would give him an idea of where the drink is.

When he got close to where it was, the woman said, "Stop playing around you're going to spill it. You are so silly."

"Yeah I'm just being silly." There was still time left, so Chris ended up just chilling and having a nice conversation with the two of them. When the time was up, the crazy woman ended up paying him for two people. Chris just shook his head and took the money. Then she gave him a hug and said, “Thanks.” She also made him hug the other person so Chris went along with it since she paid him double. Chris was just happy that this was over and he could leave. Even after he left, he still never found out who or what she was arguing with.

Gary arrived at his appointment then he went up to the door and rang the doorbell and of course, he was nervous as usual. Finally, a guy answered the door and Gary was confused. Gary thought that maybe he wrote the address down wrong. He nervously said, “I think I have the wrong address.”

The guy asked, “Are you from Cuddles?”

Gary nervously said, “Yes.”

“No, you got the right one. Come on in.”

All he could think about is what happened to Chris and woman that might have been a transgender man. He asked, “Are you a transformer?”

The guy looked at him with a really confused look in his face.

Gary said, “You know, a girl that’s really a guy but thinks he’s a girl.”

With a confused look he said, “No, me and my wife want to spice things up with our sex life. We are thinking about swinging or even maybe a threesome.”

Gary thought that the couple wanted to have a threesome with him. "I can't have sex with you guys." Then he rattled on, "It's against the rules, I'm a virgin and I wouldn't even know what to do with you. I've seen videos and it looks fun, a little messy but fun."

"We don't want to have sex with you. We are thinking about it and thought that we'd cuddle with you so that we can see how we feel about it. This way, if it's not too uncomfortable, then we could think about what we want to do next." The guy thought that they should go into the bedroom because it would resemble a couple having sex better.

Gary cuddled with his wife while the man sat in a chair in the corner. Gary glanced over at the guy. It looked like the guy was touching himself. Gary asked, "Are you touching yourself?"

The guy nervously pulled his hands out of his pants and said, "no."

After a little while, the woman told her husband to get up there and cuddle so she could see how she felt.

Gary didn't know what to do. He didn't want to cuddle with a woman, let alone a man. Especially, when he caught the man with his hand in his pants.

The guy got up there and started spooning Gary. The woman sat in the corner and started touching herself.

Gary once again asked, "Are you touching yourself?"

The woman nervously pulled her hands out of her pants and

said, "no."

After about a half hour, the couple thought that they had seen enough and paid Gary. He cuddled with two people but it only lasted about a half hour so they paid him for an hour. He was just happy to be done and leave.

While Gary was driving home, he saw Lisa. She was the girl from the appointment at the house with the bikers. She was sitting at an outdoor café and reading a book. Gary stopped, acted like he just happened to be stopping there and surprised to see her. Gary said, "Hey there, remember me?"

"Yes, I remember you. How could I forget a cute face like that?" she replied.

Gary got a happy feeling when she said that.

"Would you like to sit down?" He sat down and they talked for a little while. Then she asked, "How's the cuddling business and the electronics store going?"

"I just left an appointment. It was a couple that wanted to spice up their sex life."

Lisa asked, "What?"

"Well you know, they wanted to swing or have a threesome." He was a little embarrassed talking to Lisa about this but did it anyways.

"Did they want to swing or have a threesome with you?"

"No, they just wanted to see how it felt to lay with someone else." Lisa looked at Gary with a confused look. "Plus, I wouldn't have known what to do, I've seen videos of two people but what would the third person do?"

Lisa smiled at him and said, "Oh how cute, you're a virgin."

Gary quickly changed the subject and started talking about the electronics store. "The store has been a little slow."

"Is that good or bad?"

"It is what it is, so what are you out doing?"

"I'm taking a break because I'm moving out of my apartment to help my brother get things in order at my parents' house. He's going to move in there, so I'm going to stay there for a little while to help out. This way I could save some money since the house is paid off."

"Why don't you just sell the house and split the money?"

"The house needs a lot of work, so he's going to fix it up; and we have a lot of memories there."

Gary asked, "Not to be nosey, but do you have a job?"

"Well that was kind of being nosey."

Gary said, "I'm sorry."

"I'm just messing with you. I work at a flower shop that my parents owned. That's another reason that I'm letting my brother have the house; because I got the flower shop." They ended up having a real nice conversation and Lisa hoped that Gary would ask her out. After realizing that Gary was probably not going to, she asked him, "Would you like to go out to dinner someday?"

He said, "That would be great." They exchanged numbers and Gary told her that he would catch her later. Then he walked her to her car so that she could go home and after she left, he walked to his car so he could go home.

Dave stopped at the store to pick up a few things before he went to his appointments. Heather's ex-boyfriend Jason was walking to his car and saw Dave. Jason put his bags in the car then went back into the store. When he went in, he saw Dave hanging up a flier. Jason took the flier and put it in his pocket. He was being really careful so that Dave wouldn't see him following him around the store. Jason went to turn the corner and wasn't paying attention. A woman almost hit him with her cart so Jason hurried up to get out of the way. While he was moving out of the way, he tripped and ended up knocking over a display. He quickly and embarrassedly got up so that he wouldn't lose Dave. He went out to his car when Dave was at the register so that he could follow him when he left. After Dave paid for his things, he went out to his car and headed to his appointments. While Dave was at his appointments, Jason sat out in his car wondering what he was doing. When Dave knocked on the doors and women answered, Jason took pictures. When they were done, the women walked Dave to the door, gave him hugs and kisses on the cheek. Once again, Jason took more pictures. Jason thought that Dave was messing around with other women so he had the pictures for proof. Jason ended up following Dave to his apartment building but just kept on driving and went home.

CHAPTER 4

The next day, Dave and Gary had to work, so Chris was just hanging out at home. Then he saw a message come through so he read it. The woman sounded really nice so he messaged her back and said that he could come over right now. She was fine with that so he headed over to her house. He thought this time he may have a good woman and not a crazy one. When he got there, he went up and knocked on the door. A tall, pretty, and seemingly nice woman answered the door. Chris said, “Hi, I’m Chris from Cuddles.”

“Come on in. What size are you?” Chris was a little confused why she would ask that but told her anyways. She said, “I’ll be right back.” Now Chris was really confused so he stood there looking around and waited for her to get back. When she came back in the room, he turned around to talk to her. She was standing there with footy pajamas, a bonnet, and diaper in her hand. Then she said, "Go in the bathroom and put these on."

Chris replied, "Excuse me?"

She repeated what she said the first time. "Go in the bathroom and put these on."

By this time, he's really confused and didn't know what to do. "Let me get this right, you want me to put that on?"

"Yes."

He thought to himself, of course all women must be crazy. "You know I'm a grown man?"

"Yeah."

"If this was some crazy sexual fantasy, I'm not allowed to have sex with anyone, it's cuddling only."

"If I wanted to have sex with you, I sure wouldn't have you dress like a baby. That would be weird."

"I'm a grown man and I'm not putting that on." She just looked at him and kept holding out the clothes. Chris yelled, "OK YOU GUYS THE FUN'S ALL OVER, YOU CAN COME OUT NOW."

The woman looked at him and asked, "Whom are you talking to?"

"I know that Dave and Gary put you up to this because this can't be real.

"I don't know Dave and Gary."

Chris grabbed the stuff out of her hands and went to put them on. As he was walking away he said, "Ok I'll do it but I'm not going to be happy about it."

When he came out of the bathroom, she said, "Be a good boy and come to mommy."

Chris said, "Excuse me?"

The woman replied, "Don't make me tell you twice."

Chris hesitated and nervously walked over to her.

"Now be a good boy and sit by mommy." He sat down on the couch by her and she turned cartoons on television. She started holding him like a baby and she even gave him a bottle.

After her hour was up Chris went and put his clothes on. Then he came back out to the living room then the woman thanked him and gave him his money. Chris asked, "What was all that about?"

"I can't have children so I had my ex-boyfriends, or men that I meet at the bar, dress up like babies."

Chris regretted asking her about it and started to leave. When he was leaving, he mumbled, "That explains why you're single."

She said, "Did you say something?"

"No, I didn't say anything." Then he walked out to his car and left.

When Dave got home, Chris was just sitting on the couch watching television. He asked Chris, "How was your day off?"

"Oh, you want to know how my day was? Well, I got dressed up like a baby and some woman fed me a bottle."

Dave looked at him really weird and with a confused look.

"Well, I went to the appointment and the woman had me dress up like a baby. Apparently, she can't have kids so she dresses up the men that she meets like a baby. That's not all." He said, "she changed my diaper and burped me."

Dave sat there for a second and started laughing.

"Yeah, very funny."

"Please tell me it wasn't breast milk that you were drinking?"

"Just shut up because I'm not in the mood to listen to you right now."

"At least she used a bottle."

Chris just looked forward and shook his head.

"Oh, you want to know how my day was?" Dave said, "It was pretty good, I was a good boy and didn't dirty my diaper."

Chris just ignored for a second then said, "Don't you have a date with Heather or something?" Dave just smiled at him.

The next day at work was slow. Dave kept messing with Chris about his appointment the night before, since it wasn't that busy and he was bored. Gary was texting Lisa any chance that he could, because he'd never really talked to women before. Then Heather came walking in the store. She just got done showing a house in the area, so she stopped in to see Dave. Heather saw Gary first and started talking to him. Dave and Chris saw them talking then walked over to where they were standing.

Gary told Heather about Lisa and how they are going to go out on a date. "I met a woman and we're going on a date."

Heather replied, "That's great, I'm happy for you."

As they were talking Dave and Chris walked up. Dave wanted to change the subject so he asked Heather, "How did your showing go?"

"It went good." Then Heather looked at Gary and said, "Maybe we could go on a double date sometime and I can meet her."

Dave knew that couldn't happen anytime soon because he didn't want Lisa to say anything about the cuddling business. He knew that Heather would ask Lisa how she and Gary met. Dave said, "Maybe someday we can."

Chris took this time to get Dave back for messing with him. Chris said, "Why not tonight?"

Dave said, "I can't tonight, because I have plans."

Chris asked, "Doing what?"

Dave replied, "You know I got that one thing to do."

Heather said, "It's no big deal because I'm not feeling well and probably going to bed early anyways." Heather gave Dave a kiss on his cheek and said, "I'll talk to you later." When she turned to walk away, Dave smacked Chris in the back of the head.

After work, Gary went to pick up Lisa and they went out to dinner.

Heather had mentioned that she wasn't feeling well and was probably going to bed early. Since there was nothing going on, Dave and Chris were sitting around watching television. Chris got up to go to the bathroom so he decided to check the website. This time there was a message. Dave was really bored and Heather was home in bed so he said that he would go. The way things were going with Chris, he wasn't in a hurry to go on any appointments. Dave went to get ready so he could leave for his appointment. While Dave was driving over to his appointment Chris texted him and said, "There is a message that directly asked for you." They both were confused and wondering why they would directly ask for Dave. Then Dave figured it must have been someone that Dave cuddled with and recommended him. Dave replied, "You'll have to go to this appointment so that I can go to that one."

"That's fine, I'll go." Then he texted Dave the address to the new appointment and then left to go to his appointment.

Dave got to the house and walked up to the door. He got ready to knock and before he could, Heather opened the door. Dave was surprised to see her and wondered what was going on. Heather didn't look happy so Dave said, "I can explain." Heather didn't want to listen to it so she slammed the door in his face. Dave knocked on the door and said, "Heather, please open the door and I can explain." She wouldn't open the door or talk to him so he figured he would let her cool down then talk to her later. He was wondering how she found out, and whose house that was. When he was leaving, he noticed a realtor sign in the yard and figured out how she got the house. While this was going on, Jason was sitting down the road watching everything. Dave got to his car, turned around and looked back at the house. He was hoping that maybe Heather would open the door and come out to talk to him. Then he realized that she wasn't going to, so he got in his car and left. Jason was waiting for Dave to leave before he left, so he wouldn't see him. Before he could leave, a cop pulled up behind Jason. A neighbor called them because they didn't know what Jason was doing just sitting there. The cop noticed that he was parked in front of a fire hydrant, so he gave him a ticket for that.

As Dave was on his way home, Chris showed up at his appointment. He walked up and knocked on the door. When the door opened there was a woman standing there in a leather outfit with a whip in her hand. Chris looked at her and said, "Aw, hell no." He turned around and left. He was going to have no part of that.

When Chris got back to the apartment, he saw Dave sitting there and asked, "What's going on?" He figured that Dave shouldn't be home from his appointment yet. Chris sat down on the couch next to him.

Dave told Chris what happened. "I went to the appointment, went up to knock on the door and before I could, Heather opened it."

"How did she know?"

"I have no idea. What are you doing here, shouldn't you be at your appointment?"

"Well I knocked on the door and a dominatrix answered."

Dave just looked at him.

"I got the hell out of there; I wasn't about to get my ass kicked."

They just sat there for a few seconds then Dave asked, "Was she pretty." Chris replied, "I don't know, she had a mask on."

Dave said, "It figures."

Chris asked, "Well, what's next?"

Dave said, "I don't know." Then he got up and went into his bedroom to try to get ahold of Heather so he could try to explain what's going on. He kept calling or texting her and she wouldn't answer or text him back. He didn't know what else to do.

The next day at work, Dave told Gary about what had happened. "I went to the house, went to knock on the door and before I could, Heather opened it."

Gary had his first girlfriend so he didn't know what to say or do. He asked, "How'd this happen?"

Dave replied, "I don't know."

Gary said, "That sucks, but I'm sure you'll figure something out."

Dave replied, "I hope so."

Gary and Chris had never seen Dave like this because he'd never been this much in love with anyone. Then Chris said to Gary, "I almost got my ass kicked yesterday."

Gary said, "What?"

"Oh yeah, I went to an appointment and it was a dominatrix's house."

"Oh, a doma what?"

Chris just rolled his eyes and told him to go check the website.

Gary went and checked it to see if there were any appointments. When he checked the web site, he just closed his eyes, shook his head and let out a deep breath because they had some appointments. Gary knew it was good for business but bad for him because he's going to have to go on more appointments. He slowly walked over to Chris to tell him about the messages. They didn't know if they should say anything to Dave or not. They finally went over to where Dave was helping a customer to let him know. When he was done with the customer, they told him about the messages.

Chris said, "If you don't want to go, Gary and I will take care of them." Dave didn't want to, but knew that he had to, so he said, "I'm fine." There were appointments for that night and the next few days. They sorted them out and went on their ways.

Dave was still upset and wasn't as helpful as he normally was. Gary was trying to balance the business, work and his girlfriend. Chris was just trying to find a normal woman. They did this for the next few days.

One of Dave's appointments was at a park. Dave didn't know what it was about but went to meet her there anyways. When he got there, there was a beautiful woman probably in her fifties sitting on a blanket with a picnic basket. He walked up and introduced himself. "Hi, I'm Dave from Cuddles."

"Hi, I'm Amy, have a seat and thanks for coming. My husband passed away not too long ago. Then I saw your fliers hanging around, so I figured I'd get ahold of you and give it a try." She continued telling her story. "Me and my husband had been together since seventh grade and were high school sweethearts. We were soul mates and got married right after high school. Me and my husband used to always come to this park and have a picnic. Then we would walk over to a bench and snuggle then just look at everything. We would people watch, look at the clouds or just enjoy our time together. One day, he was diagnosed with cancer. We didn't let that stop us, we kept coming to the park. Until one day, my husband got too bad and couldn't leave the house; then shortly after that he passed away. I kept coming here by myself and doing everything that we used to do. Thanks for listening and I'm sorry if I wasted your time. If you want to leave, I understand."

"No, I'm good and I could use the company myself." Then he smiled and said, "Plus, I didn't have any dinner yet."

Amy smiled and replied, "I got some right here for you, that's if you like fried chicken?"

"That sounds great because I'm very hungry."

"So how did you get into the cuddling business? What made you decide to cuddle with strangers and listen to their problems?"

"Well, a coworker's boyfriend broke up with her and she came to me for comfort. It felt good and I could use the extra money."

Amy jokingly asked, "You're not doing it to meet women are you?"

Dave smiled and said, "No."

"So, do you have a wife or girlfriend?"

"I did, until I messed it up."

"Sorry to hear that, do you mind me asking what happened?"

"Well I met her and didn't tell her about the cuddling business because I didn't know how she would take it. Then someone took pictures of me walking in and out of women's houses and she thought that I was cheating on her with these women. I really love her and wish that she would let me explain what's going on. She still won't talk to me. A few days ago, she sent me the pictures and said to leave her alone."

"It still may work out." Amy said, "Sometimes it takes time."

"I hope, tell me some more about your husband, unless you'd rather not talk about it."

"No, I'd love to tell you about him."

Dave said, "It sounds like he was a great man and you guys really got along."

"He was, and we got along really good. Don't get me wrong, we fought like anyone else. But we just didn't let it drag on and consume our relationship. He owned his own construction company and ran it until he couldn't do it anymore. Then he sold it so I could have money to help take care of him or take care of myself when he's gone. No matter what, he always took care of me."

"I hope someday Heather and I have what you guys had."

"Don't give up, and you will." The two of them had a really nice conversation and a nice little picnic dinner. When they were done eating, they went and snuggled next to each other on the bench. They people watched, looked at the clouds and had a great time. They did exactly what Amy and her husband would do before he got too sick. They were having such a good time that they didn't realize what time it was. They ate, talked and hung out for about two hours. "Wow, just realized the time." Amy said, "I'm sorry that I kept you here this long and I have to go but I had a great time."

She went to hand Dave some money and Dave refused to take it. "Your company was a good enough payment."

"No, here." Then she went to hand him the money again but once again he refused to take it. Amy gave Dave a big hug and said, "thanks."

Then Dave walked Amy to her car then said, "thanks for the food and the great conversation. I hope I didn't bore you with my relationship problems?"

"You didn't and you're a great guy, I hope everything works out for you."

Dave said, "Maybe we can do this again?"

Amy replied, "That would be great." Then they both left to go home.

A few weeks had passed and the business was doing well. Heather still wouldn't talk to Dave, and he still really missed her. He had been trying to get ahold of her since the day she quit talking to him. Dave continued to go to the park with Amy, and continued to do what they've been doing.

Then one day Gary and Lisa came over to the apartment. Gary seemed a little weirder than he normally was. All of a sudden, he said, "I can't hold it in anymore, we're getting married."

Dave and Chris were shocked to hear that, and

congratulated the two of them. Dave and Chris would have to pick up some of the slack because Gary had a wedding to help plan for.

Lisa asked Dave, “Have you talked to Heather since you broke up?”

“No, but I’ve been trying.”

“Do you want me to say something to her?”

“Thanks, but I don’t think that would work either.”

“It might not work if Lisa talked to her, but it might work if you could get the women that you cuddled with to talk to her.” Gary said, “Let them explain that you never slept with them and helped most of them with their problems.”

Chris said, “That might just work.”

Dave wanted her back and at this point would try anything. The four of them went to talk to these women and see if they would help Dave out.

The next day, Dave went over to Heather’s house. Every time he went over there, she wouldn’t answer the door. She would just yell from inside the house for him to go away. Dave would turn around and leave but this time he didn’t leave. “I love and miss you. I’m not leaving until you let me explain what’s going on, then if you want me to leave I will.” This time she opened the door to hear what Dave had to say. When she opened it, there was Dave, Chris, Gary, Lisa and the women that he cuddled with. “I didn’t sleep with any of these women, they just wanted someone to cuddle with and talk to.

That's all the business is, it's a cuddling business and that's it. It has nothing to do with sex."

Then everyone else started speaking up and defending Dave. They explained what he did for them, like helping them cope with a death, make up with a significant other or just get through any bad times that they were having.

Then Amy spoke up and told Heather about the times that she and Dave spent together. "Since my husband passed away, I never thought I'd be happy, but Dave made me feel happiness again. We still meet up, and he can't quit talking about you. Dave really loves you and if you love him, don't let this ruin what you have, because he may not always be there. Me and my husband didn't always get along, we had our differences, but I would do anything to be able to tell him that I love him and hold him one more time."

Heather started to cry then gave Dave a big hug and kiss. They told each other that they loved each other.

"I should've told you about the business a long time ago. I really liked you and didn't know how you would take it; I didn't want to mess anything up." Then he asked, "How did you find out about the business anyways?"

"Jason found out and he followed you around taking pictures."

Then Jason pulled up in his car and walked up there to see what was going on. "WHAT'S GOING ON?" Jason yelled, "HE'S

CHEATING ON YOU AND HE'S NO GOOD FOR YOU. YOU DESERVED BETTER THAN THAT."

Heather got tired of hearing it and slapped Jason. Then she said, "I never want to see you again, stay out of my life."

Jason was embarrassed about what happened and left.

Dave looked at Heather and said, "Remind me never to piss you off." Then they hugged and kissed again.

CHAPTER 5

Weeks have passed, Dave and Heather are doing great. Dave continued to go to the park and meet up with Amy like he had been for many weeks before. It's just that instead of a picnic for two, it's a picnic for three. Heather's been going with him because Amy insisted that she go.

Once in a while Chris, Gary, and Lisa would go to the park and hang out with them too. Heather said, "I'm fine with the business, but promise me that there's no sex involved and will never be involved."

"I love you and promise."

Chris knew the issues that Heather and Dave had so he decided to handle most of the appointments. This way they could have more time to themselves and he had better chances at normal women. He was also hoping that he might find his special woman someday.

Since Gary was still living with his mom, he and Lisa moved in together. They would go over to his mom's to visit and let her help out with the wedding arrangements. The wedding day was coming real soon.

The day before the wedding Dave, Chris, and Gary went to the club. Heather, Amy, and Lisa hung out together for a women's night out. It was Gary's last day as a free man. The three of them laughed, drank and had a great time. They were standing by the bar when the couple that Gary cuddled with came by. They stopped to say hi and talk to Gary for a little bit. They said, "Hey there!"

Gary replied, "How are you guys, what are you two out doing?"

"We're meeting some new friends up here."

"I'm getting married tomorrow so we're just up here having a few drinks."

Then the couple congratulated Gary and went to meet up with their new friends.

Dave asked, "Who was that?"

He was a little embarrassed still so he just said, "They're some people that I met."

The entertainment for the night was a local rapper and DJ.

All of a sudden in between songs, he wanted to congratulate Gary on his wedding day. Gary and Dave were a little surprised and wondered how he knew.

"I saw him in the restroom and told him that one of my best friends is getting married tomorrow." Chris said, "then I asked him if he could say something." The three of them kept drinking, talking, and having a good time.

Then toward the end of the night, the rapper went to the bar to get a drink. He looked over at Dave and Gary and asked, "Which one of you are getting married?"

Gary said, "I am."

"Congratulations and let me buy you a shot." Then he looked at the three of them and asked, "Did you work at the electronics store?"

They said, "Yes."

"You guys looked familiar, I think I bought my first set of DJ equipment from there." Then he went on his way.

A drunk guy at the bar said to Gary, "So you're getting married?"

Gary replied, "Yes."

"Do you want a beer?"

"Yeah, I'll take a beer."

Then the guy took a drink out of his beer, looked at it and handed it to Gary. Then he turned to walk away and tripped over a barstool. Gary sat the beer down and asked, "Are you ok?"

The next day was Gary's big day. He was a little hung over but managed to make it there. He was getting cold feet, but Dave and Chris were there for support. He was also a little nervous of Lisa's brother and biker club. Gary's side of the church was his family and friends, while Lisa's side was the whole biker gang. Since her parents passed away, the biker gang was her family now.

As the ceremony was taking place, Dave and Heather kept looking over at each other and smiling.

Chris just sat there looking at Dave and shaking his head.

After Gary and Lisa were married, they jumped on the back of some motorcycles and rode to the reception. During the reception, they were all standing around talking.

Chris asked, "What are you doing for your honeymoon?"

"We're going to wait a little bit because we have some stuff to take care of first. Then we'll figure something out and a place to go." It turned out to be a great night. Gary and Lisa were married, Dave and Heather's relationship was doing great and Chris caught the bouquet.

The next day, there was a message on the website. Gary was with his wife and Dave was at Heather's, so Chris was the only one there to go. He wasn't doing anything so he decided to go on the appointment. He got ready then drove over to the house. He went to the door and knocked, then the door opened and it was Lucy. She was the transgender man or ugly woman from before. Chris said, "Really, you don't live here."

Lucy said, "Yes I do, I just moved here."

Chris thought what the hell because he wasn't going to argue with this woman again. When his time was up Chris left and went home.

A few minutes after he left, there was a knock on the door. It was Dave and Gary. They handed Lucy some money and she handed them a video camera. Dave looked at Gary and said, "Proof, my ass." They both laughed then hi fived each other. It turned out that Lucy didn't live there and it was a house for sale. Dave had Heather get the key so they could set Chris up. Gary put the video on a cd.

The next day at the electronics store, Chris came walking in and everyone was laughing and giggling at him. He didn't know what was going on. He looked up at the televisions then saw the video of him cuddling and arguing with Lucy.

Heather and Lisa didn't want to miss this, so they were there to watch. Dave, Gary, Heather and Lisa were standing there laughing. Chris looked over at them and said, "Ha ha, very funny." Then he took off into the back to take out the cd.

Dave said to Gary, "You made extra copies, right?"

Gary smiled and said, "Of course." They all stood there with smiles on their faces.

-CUDDLES-

VOLUME 2

CHAPTER 6

While Dave, Gary, Heather and Lisa were standing there, Heather said to Lisa, "Well that was enough fun for me, are you ready?"

Dave asked, "What are you two doing?"

Heather replied, "What women do best, shop."

Dave said, "Good thing I have two jobs because I could never afford you."

Heather smiled and replied, "Don't worry about that because I have my own money. If I needed any from you, I'd ask."

Lisa said to Gary, "We're married, so you're screwed."

Dave said, "She's right."

Heather gave Dave a kiss while Lisa gave Gary a kiss, and then the two of them left. Then Gary asked Dave, "Did you tell Chris that you were moving out yet?"

Dave answered, "No, I will tonight."

Gary asked, "How do you think he's going to take it?"

"Probably not good but I can always borrow the footy pajamas and bottle from that one woman." Dave and Gary both laughed then went on with their day.

When the day ended, Dave went home to talk to Chris about him moving out. He didn't tell him right away. He bought a twelve-pack of beer on the way home and thought he'd ease into it. Finally, Dave thought we're both adults here so he said, "I'm moving in with Heather."

Chris asked, "How long have you known about this?"

"Not too long." He said, "We discussed it after we had our little break up."

"Well, you better hope this is what you want. If you leave then you may not be able to come back. I've been thinking about working out and your room may be my new workout area."

Dave said, "We'll still be best friends, we have the cuddling business and we still work together at the electronics store. Plus, I've been thinking about working out myself, maybe I'll come over and work out with you."

"You know that that's not going to happen." Chris replied, "I have no plans on working out, I was just trying to trick you into staying."

"I've known you all my life, I knew that wasn't going to happen. You'll be fine. I'll help you out with your rent until you get on your feet. Heather and I will have you over for dinner sometime."

"Is Heather a good cook?" Chris asked, "You know that there are certain foods that I don't like or can't eat." Then Chris started to rattle on and said, "I just don't want my throat swelling up or you having to do the Heimlich maneuver."

Dave replied, "First off, those are two different things and second, you're not allergic to anything."

Chris said, "Yeah, I was just trying to trick you into staying again. I just wish you the best. I'm glad you found someone like Heather because you deserve it."

Dave replied, "Now that I'm moving out, maybe you can find a woman like Heather." Then they hugged and Dave went to start moving out.

Nine Months Later . . .

A little over nine months after Dave moved out, they received a message that asked specifically for Dave. They were at work when they saw it. It was Cindy, the woman that was fighting with her girlfriend. He figured that they were fighting over something stupid again then he would go over there and tell her that she wrong again, then the fight would be over. Shortly after they got the message, Dave got a text from Heather. Heather was pregnant and going into labor. He hurried to find Chris and tell him about the text. Dave said, “Heather’s going into labor and you’re going to have to go on the appointment.”

Chris instantly responded, “It’s funny how you move out and almost exactly to the day, Heather’s having a baby.”

“Well, it was a new beginning for us.” Dave said, “Also it was a new bed that we bought so we wanted to break it in, then there was the time in the kitchen, living room, and the garage, before the bed.”

“Really?” Chris replied, “Go, I got it.”

Dave said, “Thanks.” Then he explained the situation that had happened before about the woman. “Just go there, tell her she’s wrong, they love each other, and everything will be fine. Then they will both cuddle up next to you on the couch. Like I said, they are probably fighting over something stupid or they both just really missed me.” Dave said with a smile.

“Whatever, and don’t you got somewhere to be?” Chris replied, “I’m no baby expert but I do believe that there’s a time limit on these things.”

Dave said, “Yeah I better go.”

Gary wasn’t working, so Dave texted him to tell him that Heather was going into labor. Dave left to go to the hospital and Chris finished his shift. When he got off, he went home to get ready for his appointment. He drove over to Cindy's house and knocked on the door. Cindy answered the door and Chris told her who he was. He said, "Hi, I'm Chris from Cuddles."

She just looked at him and said, "You're not Dave, where's Dave?"

Chris said, "Dave's girlfriend is going into labor, so he couldn't make it." Then he rattled on, "Apparently he moved out nine months ago and decided that they had to have sex in every room of the house, on every new appliance they bought."

With a confused look she said, "OK whatever, well, I guess you'll have to do, come on in and have a seat." As they were walking to the couch she continued, "No offense about you'll have to do, and that's sweet for Dave, he's such a nice guy."

With a sarcastic look on his face he responded, "None taken." Then he sarcastically mumbled to himself, "Dave's such a nice guy."

They walked over and sat down on the couch, then they talked. Chris sat there with an irritated look on his face because she kept talking and asking questions about Dave. She asked, "So, Dave's going to be a dad?"

Chris replied, "Yes."

Then she asked, "That is so sweet, he'll be a great dad, don't you think?"

Chris sarcastically answered, "Yes, he'll be a great dad."

"So, what is Dave's girlfriend like?"

"She's nice."

"That's good because Dave's . . ."

Before she could finish, Chris interrupted her and said, "We all know, because Dave's such a nice guy. He's such a nice guy that since he moved out last minute, he's going to help me out until I get on my feet."

"Well that was nice of him to help you out."

Chris rolled his eyes and said, "Yeah it was nice of him."

The whole time that they were talking Cindy was looking and acting like she was waiting for someone or something. Shortly after they sat on the couch, Nikki walked in and started yelling at her. She yelled, "WHO THE HELL IS THIS?"

Chris panicked and said, "You were wrong, you love each other, and everything will be fine."

By this time, the two women had already been arguing. Then Nikki jumped on the couch and started trying to fight with Cindy. Chris was sitting there with two women fighting over top of him. He's trying to break it up and finally succeeded. He got them apart and tried to mediate what's going on between them. He stood there with his shirt ripped and red marks on his face, while the two women kept arguing. Chris said to Cindy, "Hold on." While he turned to try to calm Nikki down, she went to hit Cindy, but hit Chris. When she hit him, she knocked him out and he fell on the floor. Then Cindy and

Nikki freaked out and dropped to their knees to see if Chris was ok.

Cindy said to her girlfriend, "He's right; we do love each other, everything will be fine, and we do need to stop fighting over stupid stuff."

Nikki replied. "I love you."

Finally, Chris came to and the women helped him on the couch while they apologized for hitting him. When he was ok to leave, they paid him for his trouble and gave him a big tip for beating him up. As he was leaving, the women said, "Tell Dave we said hi."

Then Cindy said, "Tell him congratulations on the baby."

"Dave's having a baby?" Nikki asked. "I love babies and he's going to be a great dad." Chris just rolled his eyes and shook his head, then continued to his car.

When Chris left the women's house, he went straight up to the hospital to see how Dave and Heather were doing. When he got there, he texted Dave to tell him that he was there. He went into the waiting room to wait for Dave to come and get him. As he was sitting in the waiting room, nurses kept asking him if he was waiting to see a doctor? That was because his face had red marks and his clothes were a mess. Finally, Dave came into the waiting room to meet Chris. When he walked into the waiting room, he saw Chris sitting there looking like a mess. Dave asked him, "What happened?"

"Well, I don't know whose fault it was, if they love each other, and it's probably not going to be alright. I was sitting there talking to one woman then the other woman came home and they started fighting. Then I tried to calm them down and got hit."

Dave asked, "You got beat up by two women?" Then he started laughing.

"Yeah yeah, keep laughing. All I know is the one woman must be a boxer or MMA fighter because I know that she's not bagging groceries for a living."

Dave said, "Yeah whatever, let's go see the baby." Then they walked up to the room Heather was in.

When they got up to the room Amy was already there. Amy said to Chris, "What happened to you?"

Chris replied, "Nothing."

Amy said, "Well it looks like you got hit by a bus."

Then Dave said, "Chris got beat up by two women."

"I didn't get beat up, I turned around and got hit. I basically got sucker punched."

As they were sitting there talking, Gary texted Dave and said that they were on their way up to the hospital. Dave texted him and told him what room Heather was in. When they got there, Lisa freaked out about the baby and had to hurry up to hold her. Lisa exclaimed, "WHERE'S THE BABY?" Then she went and held the baby and asked, "So, what name did you decide on?"

Heather replied, "Anna."

Then Dave told Gary about Chris's appointment with the

lesbians. “Oh yeah, Chris got beat up by two women.”

Gary asked, “What?”

Dave replied, “He literally got beat up by two women.”

Of course, Chris didn’t like it and replied, “Really, you just had to say something?”

Dave and Gary sat there laughing. Lisa didn’t know what was going on so she asked Heather, “What’s so funny?”

Heather said, “Chris got beat up by a couple of girls.” Then all three women started laughing and now everyone in the room was laughing, except Chris.

Chris said, “I’m glad that I can entertain you guys.” Then he said in a sarcastic voice, “Plus, they were women not girls.” All that did was make everyone laugh again. “Go ahead and keep laughing, I’m not going to beat up any girls.”

Dave looked at him laughing and asked, “Were they women, or girls?”

Chris replied “really?” Dave just looked at Chris then started pointing at his shirt and face.

Gary whispered to Dave, “What’s the difference between women and girls? Aren’t they basically the same?”

Dave looked at Gary and shook his head. Then he said, “I was being sarcastic.”

Heather asked Lisa, “Did you hear about the transgender guy that Chris cuddled with?”

Lisa replied, “Guy?”

Chris said with a sarcastic smile “OK, enough about me, how’s the baby? And for the record, it might have been a real ugly woman instead of a man.” Everyone laughed.

Chris, Gary, Lisa and Amy left to go home. Chris and Gary had to work in the morning. The next day at work, Chris and Gary were just standing around talking. “What was the big deal about getting beat up by a girl?” Gary said, “I’ve been beat up by a girl before.” Gary continued to tell Chris about getting beat up by a girl. “I was in fifth grade and went to get the last swing that wasn’t being used. Then Mary decided she wanted the swing, so she came up and pushed me down, then took the swing.”

Chris just sat there with a puzzled or confused look on his face the whole time Gary was talking. “I didn’t get beat up by a girl; and if I did, at least it wouldn’t be over no stupid swing. Plus, I had two full grown women fighting and I was the man that had to break it up. If I wanted, I could’ve beat both them up, but I’m not hitting a woman. Now if you don’t shut up, I’m going to have Mary come push your ass down again. Let’s go check the computer.” Then Chris stopped and said, “By the way, never tell that story to anyone ever again.” Then they walked over to check the website to see if they have any appointments.

There were three messages and they were all for that day. Chris and Gary didn’t know if they should tell Dave or just do them on their own. They decided to text Dave anyways to let him know. Dave said, “I’ll take one because I could use a break from this hospital.”

They all met up at Chris’ apartment to sort out the appointments. Lisa went up to the hospital to stay with Heather while Gary and Dave went to their appointments. Dave took the earliest appointment so that he could get back up to the hospital. The message already explained everything that was going on. It was an old woman that didn’t have much time to live. Her husband had passed years before and she had no other family. The only family that she had was the other people in the nursing home or the staff. She really never said much to anyone or left her room too often because she felt that her life was over since she lost her husband. The nursing staff thought that it would be nice to have someone come and spend some time with her before she passed. They asked her if it would be ok if they contacted Cuddles and had someone come over. She wasn’t feeling good but she shook her head motioning yes.

When Dave got there, he went to the front counter and told them who he was. The receptionist called the nurse that messaged them. The nurse came walking up. “Hi, I’m Kim.” She said, “thanks for coming.”

Dave replied, “I’m Dave and it’s no problem.” Dave and Kim shook hands.

Kim said, “Follow me.” Then she started walking Dave to the woman’s room. As they were walking to her room Kim and Dave talked. Kim asked, “Are you sure this isn’t a problem?”

Dave said, “No, not at all.”

“Her name is Betty and like I said in the message, she has no family since her husband passed away years ago. She’s not doing good and hopefully this will make her feel like she’s not alone.”

“I’ll see what I can do.”

Dave walked into the room and introduced himself to Betty. He said, “Hi, I’m Dave; can I come in?” She just laid in her bed and didn’t say anything. Dave sat in the chair next to her bed and started talking to her. “I’m sorry about your husband and that you’re not feeling well. The nurse said that you don’t get out of your room too often.” She just laid there and didn’t say anything. He asked, “Is it OK if I lay down next to you?” This time she shook her head yes. He laid next to her and talked to her. Even though she wasn’t talking back he kept talking to her. He told her about Heather and baby Anna. “I just had a baby girl and her name is Anna. Her mom’s name is Heather and she’s a beautiful woman that I hope I spend the rest of my life with.” He told her about Amy and how they became good friends. “The main reason that me and my friends started the cuddling business was because no one should be alone. This way if someone needs someone to talk to or just someone to snuggle up to, they can message us.” He tried to make her feel at home or that she was loved. "It's also a good way to meet new people. I met a woman named Amy and she's turning out to be a really good friend. She lost her husband, and I'm glad that I can help her get through it. As a matter of fact, she helped me get through an issue that me and Heather were having." He talked to her like they'd known each other all their lives. When the time was up, he said, "Thanks for letting me spend time with you and for listening to me." He got up and started to walk towards the door.

Then Betty spoke for the first time. "Thanks, and that was nice of you to come to a complete stranger and make her feel like family. I don't have any family anymore, and for years felt alone. Hold on to Heather and especially that precious little baby. You never know when it will all come to an end."

Dave walked back to the bed where Betty was laying and gave her a kiss on her forehead.

She looked at him with a big smile and said, "God bless you, you're a very special young man."

When Dave walked out of the room, Kim came up and thanked him again. "Thanks, and how did it go?"

"It went great, she is a great and smart woman. She didn't say much but when she did, it meant a lot to me."

"She is a great woman and thanks again." She went to pay him some money and he refused to take it.

Dave asked, "If it's ok with you and Betty, I'd like to stop back by if I get a little free time?"

"I think that would be great, and I'm sure Betty won't care."

Here's my number, keep me updated on how Betty's doing." Then he gave Kim his number so she could keep him updated on Betty's health. He left so that he could get up to the hospital.

While Dave was at his appointment with Betty, Chris and Gary were on the way to their appointments. Gary arrived at his appointment, then he walked up and knocked on the door. A pretty middle-aged woman answered the door. She had a nice house and was dressed nicely so Gary figured that she was doing well for herself. He introduced himself, "Hi, I'm Gary from Cuddles."

The woman politely said, "Come on in and have a seat." They walked over to the couch and Gary sat down. Then she asked, "Would you like a glass of tea or lemonade?"

Gary answered, "I'll take a glass of lemonade." Then she stood there staring at him. Gary was getting a little uncomfortable. Then she asked, "I will take a glass of lemonade, what?"

Gary asked, "Please?"

"Sure, you can have a glass of lemonade. Well I'm going to go and get us some drinks, I'll be right back. Don't go running away," she jokingly said. Then she walked into the kitchen to get their drinks. Gary was a little confused by this woman because he didn't know how to take her. She seemed really nice and polite but the whole please thing confused him. The woman came back into the living room and handed Gary his drink. Then she went back into the kitchen for something. This woman seemed a little odd so Gary was scared to drink his lemonade, so he sat it down on the coffee table. Then the woman came back into the room and sat down on the couch with her drink. She just stared at the glass of lemonade on the coffee table. Gary kept looking back at her and the drink on the table. She finally took a deep breath and grabbed a coaster then sat her drink down on it. Then she picked up Gary's glass and set a coaster underneath it. She said, "That's ok, not everyone is raised with manners." By this time Gary was scared of this lady.

The woman stood up, walked over and turned on some old fifties music. Then she walked back over to the couch and cuddled up next to Gary. She said, "I really enjoy listening to music while I cuddle because it calms me down and it's relaxing." While they were cuddling, she kept moving around like she couldn't get comfortable. She stood up then told Gary, "Stand up." She took a deep breath and started fluffing the cushions on the couch. Now Gary was terrified of this lady. When she was done, she said, "sit." Gary didn't hesitate; he sat down and stared straight ahead. Then she started talking to him like nothing happened. "Now we're good. I'm glad that you didn't leave because I didn't want to have to go and find you."

Gary asked, "Find me?"

"Yes, get in my car and drive around looking for you. What else would it mean?"

Gary knew that this woman was obviously crazy and just wanted his time to be up. He asked, “So were you married?”

“I don’t talk about that.”

Then he asked, “Do you have any children?”

“I don’t talk about that either.” Gary decided to just sit there and if she said something, he would just reply back to her. He felt scared and very uncomfortable the whole time. She looked at Gary and said, “You haven’t touched your lemonade. That’s wasteful, and we’re not wasteful around here.” Gary didn’t know what to do because he was scared to drink it. He was also scared of her, so he picked it up and slammed it. She said, “now wasn’t that good?”

Gary replied, “Yes.”

The woman asked, “how long have you been cuddling with women for?”

“For almost a year and a half.”

“Apparently you haven’t found the right woman yet.”

“Right woman?”

“You know, someone to spend the rest of your life with.”

“Yeah I did, I’ve been married for almost a year.”

The woman stared straight ahead, took a deep breath and shook her head. Then said, “Apparently she’s not the right one or you wouldn’t be going out on these cuddling dates.”

Gary was confused and asked, “Dates?”

“Why else would you go to a woman’s house and cuddle if

you're not trying to meet someone or get laid?"

"I don't do it for those reasons."

"Well it don't matter because I'm not that easy and I think our time is up." The woman got up and grabbed the glasses off the coffee table, then walked into the kitchen. Gary was thinking about leaving like he did before but he was scared to, because this woman might actually chase him down. Then after a few seconds she walked back into the living room and paid Gary.

Gary stood up said, "I had a great time, and thanks for the lemonade." Then he got out of there as fast as he could.

Chris drove to his appointment and when he got there, there was a bunch of kids running around the yard. He was wondering if he had the right address. He decided he would walk up to the house and see. As he was walking up to the house, two little girls came running up, asking him questions. A little girl asked, "are you here to see my mommy?"

Chris replied, "Yes."

Another little girl asked, "Are you going to be our new daddy?"

Chris answered, "No, I'm just here to talk to your mommy."

Then she asked, "Why, don't you like kids?"

He answered, "Yeah, I like kids."

Then the other girl asked, "Do you have kids?"

Chris replied, "No."

Then the other girl asked, "Can we play with them?"

He replied, "I don't have any kids."

Then she asked, "why not, don't you like them?"

He replied, "No, I mean; yes, I like kids." Then a little boy was standing there picking his nose. Chris asked, "Now that's gross, you're not going to eat that, are you?" The little boy just shrugged his shoulders. Then another boy walked up and started hitting him with a toy bat. Chris said, "Ouch, you really shouldn't be hitting people with bats."

Then a woman came to the door and yelled at the kids to leave him alone then said to go play. She asked, "are you from Cuddles?"

Chris answered, "Yeah, I'm Chris." She said, "come in, and I'm sorry for my kids bugging you."

"It's fine, kids will be kids."

"Do you have any kids?"

"No, would you like to reschedule?"

"No, it's fine, unless you do."

"I'm good." Even though he really didn't want to because her kids were running around.

She said, "I need a break with another adult because these kids are driving me nuts, come over here and have a seat." Then walked over and sat on the couch. She asked, "Would you like something to drink?"

"I'm good."

"So how was your day?"

"It was good, I'd ask how yours was, but I'm sure with all these kids it was pretty busy."

"Yeah it usually is." Then the oven timer started going off. "I'll be right back." Then she walked into the kitchen. When she left to go into the kitchen, the kids came into the house. One of them ran up and started shooting Chris with a toy dart gun. Chris, with a fake smile, blew it off and told him to go play. "You better go play before your mom comes back and yells at you." Then a little girl came up to him and handed him her doll. The doll was all wet. Chris asked, "Why is your doll all wet?"

The little girl replied, "It fell into the toilet." Chris with a disgusted look held the doll up with his thumb and first finger. Then the woman came back into the room, told the kids to go eat, then apologized to Chris.

Then she sat down on the couch next to him then cuddled up to him as they watched television and talked. She said, "I love my kids to death but it's not easy doing this basically on my own."

"What about their dad, is he in the picture?"

"He left when I was pregnant with our fifth child. He moved out of the state so they don't see him too much but he really doesn't want anything to do with them anyways."

"It's probably better that way, especially if he doesn't care to see them. Does he pay child support or do you have a job?"

"Yes he does, because he knows he'll go to jail if he didn't and I work at a grocery store."

"Do you have family or friends that help you out? I'm sorry if I'm being nosy.

"You're fine and yes I do, I couldn't make it without them."

"That's good."

As her kids were finishing up their food, she went into the kitchen to take care of their plates.

The kids went outside when they were done, except for one. He walked over to the couch and started jumping on it. Chris said, "OK that's enough and I don't think your mom's going to like you jumping on the couch." The kid just kept doing it and didn't say a word. Chris said, "Ok then, your mom will come in here and beat your butt for jumping on the couch."

The kid quickly jumped off the couch, took off running and yelled, "MOM THE MAN SAID BUTT!"

The woman finished up in the kitchen then walked back into the living room. She asked, "What did he say?"

"He came over then started jumping on the couch and I told him that you'll beat his butt, then he yelled mom the man said butt."

"I'm sorry."

"That's fine, he's just a kid and was having fun." The woman's time was up and she was going to go to get some money to pay Chris. He said, "Don't worry about it, you're a single parent talking care of these kids."

"No, it's fine. I got the money."

"keep it, I'm not taking your money."

"Thanks." The woman gave Chris a big hug and walked him to the door.

Chris started to walk to his car and her kids all ran up to him then started throwing water balloons at him. Chris just stopped and stood there while they threw the balloons at him. Then asked, "Are you done?"

One of the kids yelled, "NO!"

He turned around to see what was going on and the kid threw the balloon at him.

He hit Chris in the forehead with the balloon. The kid said, "Now I'm done."

Chris looked at the kid, then turned around and walked to his car. When he left, he headed up to the hospital to meet up with everyone.

CHAPTER 7

When Chris got up to the hospital Gary was already in the room telling everyone about his appointment. When Chris walked into the room Dave asked, “Well, Gary had quite the adventure, how did your appointment go?”

Chris explained, “Well, the woman was nice, and pretty.”

Heather replied, “Well, that sounds like it went well.”

Chris said, “That part was good, but . . .”

Then Dave interrupted him and said, “She had a penis.”

“No, she didn’t have a penis. At least a penis wouldn’t ask a million questions, hit me with a bat, shoot me in the head with a gun, hand me a doll that was in the toilet or throw water balloons at me.” Everyone looked at him with a confused look and wondered what he was talking about. “She had kids.”

Gary said, "Well it sounds like she had a penis because it sounds like you got fucked."

Chris replied, "So you got jokes?"

Dave said, "Well, that was pretty good."

Then the girls both agreed and said, "That was pretty good."

As he was done telling everyone what happened, Dave got a phone call. He went out into the hallway to answer it. It was the nurse from the nursing home. She asked, "Dave?"

"Yes, this is Dave."

"This is Kim from the nursing home."

"Hey how are you doing?"

"Well, not to good, Betty passed away."

Dave sat there for a second and thought about what she had told him. Then said, "I'm sorry."

"Thanks, but I deal with a lot of this in my line of work."

"Thanks for calling. Are they going to have a funeral for her?"

"No because she doesn't have any family so they'll probably just bury her next to her husband."

"When you find out, can you call me to tell me where and when?"

"Yeah, I'll let you know."

"Thanks again."

"No problem."

Dave walked back into the room and looked upset. Heather asked, "What was that about?"

"Betty, the woman from the nursing home, passed away." Everyone told him that they were sorry. Dave walked over to Heather then gave her a big hug and said, "I love you."

Lisa walked up to Gary, gave him a big hug and kiss.

Chris didn't have anyone to hug or kiss. He just said, "Don't worry about me, I can feel all the love in here."

Then all of them except for Heather went and gave Chris a group hug. Heather was in bed so she couldn't get up to hug him. She said, "Even though you can be a pain in the ass, I love you too."

"I'm taking that like you meant that in a good way."

The next day all three of them had to work. Dave could've taken the day off, but he figured he could use the money. He also felt bad for Betty and thought that working might help him get it off his mind. Chris and Gary knew that Dave had a lot going on so they let him be. That way he could handle Betty's passing the way that he wanted or needed to. Heather was coming home that day, so Lisa said that she would go and pick her up from the hospital. That way she didn't have to wait for Dave to get off work or him to be bothered by something else. Even though he had no ties with Betty, he felt really bad that she passed away all alone. He was just glad that he could have the opportunity to make her feel loved and not alone. Gary kept checking for messages and they had nothing for the night. When they got off work, they all went home to enjoy their afternoons.

Since there were no appointments, Chris was sitting around watching television when all of a sudden, his phone started ringing. Chris picked up his phone and saw that it was Dave calling, so he answered it to see what he wanted. Dave asked, "do you want to go and get a few drinks?" Heather knew that Dave had a lot going on and thought that it would be nice for him to go out for a little bit.

Chris had nothing else going on so he said, "yeah I could use a few drinks."

Dave called Gary before he called Chris, to see if he wanted go, but he already had plans. He and Lisa were taking his mom out to dinner. Dave still had to get ready, because he called Gary and Chris as soon as he got done talking with Heather. Dave said, "I'll be over to pick you up after I get out of the shower and get done eating."

Chris replied, "that's fine because I have to shower and eat too."

When they arrived at the club they hung out at the bar, talked and listened to the music. As they were standing there two beautiful women came up and started talking to them. One of the women said, "Hi I'm Ashley and this is Tori."

Chris said, "Hi, I'm Chris and this is Dave."

Dave felt a little uncomfortable because Heather was at

home with the baby.

Ashley said, “Hey we’ll be right back because we have to go to the little girls’ room.”

When they left Chris said, “Settle down and don’t ruin this for me. You’re doing nothing wrong, all you’re doing is talking. It’s not like you’re sleeping with any of them.”

Dave thought maybe this was Chris’ chance to meet someone, so he figured that he would play along. Dave said, “I’ll talk but if they want to leave with us then that’s it and I’m done.”

Chris replied, “That’s fine.” The women came back then Chris bought them some drinks and they hung out together talking.

While they were standing there talking Ashley asked, “so what do you guys do for a living?”

Dave got ready to tell her that they worked at the electronics store, but before he could, Chris interrupted him. He said, “we work for an accounting firm.”

Dave just looked at Chris with a confused look.

Chris looked back at Dave as to say, just go along with it.

“Accounting huh?” Tori said, “So you must be doing really well for yourselves.”

Dave looked at Chris, then he looked at Dave and said, “Yes, we do pretty good.”

Ashley asked, “Do you guys have girlfriends?”

Chris looked at Dave and got ready to say that he didn’t but

Dave did, then Dave replied, "No." He thought that this might be a chance that Chris could meet someone and didn't want to ruin it. Even though he did, and was in love with Heather. Everything seemed to be going really good and Dave started loosening up. Dave was actually having a good time too even though he kept thinking about Heather. They sat there for a couple of hours drinking and talking. After a while, Dave kept trying to leave; but every time he'd bring it up, the women would insist on one more drink.

Chris was drunk at this time so he would side with the women. One time, Chris said to Dave, "Quit being a little bitch."

Dave blew it off because he knew that Chris was drunk. Dave left to go to the bathroom and Tori distracted Chris so that Ashley could put something in his drink. When he got back, he grabbed his drink and finished it. Dave once again tried to leave, but everyone insisted on another drink. Dave and Chris had to work in the morning so he just wanted to leave. Dave said, "This is our last one because we have to work in the morning."

Ashley said, "Ok fine then, you go ahead and be a party pooper." Then she went to order more drinks. All of a sudden Dave started feeling weird. Now all of a sudden, he felt like he was drunk. He had to use the restroom again so Ashley helped him to the restroom. By this time Chris was wasted and made a stupid comment like he usually did when he's drinking. "Why do they call it the restroom, there's no chairs or beds in there." He kept rattling on about the restroom. "Maybe it's called the restroom because I fell asleep on the toilet before." He was too drunk to realize that Dave never came back.

The next day, Dave woke up in a motel room lying next to the girl from the club. He didn't remember driving there, how he got there, or anything that happened the night before. All he could think about was Heather and wondering what he was going to tell her. She left a bunch of messages and texts wondering where he was or if he was ok. Dave got up out of bed and put his clothes on, then left. He tried calling Chris, but he wouldn't wake up so he drove over to his apartment. He banged on the door but he still wouldn't wake up. Dave thought that he would try to open the door and it was unlocked so opened right up. Dave thought that Chris must have been really drunk because he never locked his door when he got home. Dave went over to the couch were Chris was sleeping and woke him up. Chris was still wearing the clothes that he had on from the night before and was really hung over. Dave asked, "what happened last night?"

"Am I dead?"

"No, you're not dead but what happened last night?"

"I don't know. We were talking to two women and then you woke me up."

"That's all you remember?"

"Yes."

"Well I woke up in bed with a strange woman."

"That's not good, especially if you don't remember because you don't know if she was any good or not."

"That's the last thing I'm worried about. I need to figure out something to tell Heather. I'm just going to tell her that I passed out here because I shouldn't have been driving." Then Dave left to run home to get ready for work so Chris could get ready.

When Chris got to work, Gary came up to him to see what happened last night. Gary said, "Man you look like shit, what's going on?"

"I don't know. I don't remember anything."

"Heather's been calling me all night to see if I heard from you two." Then shortly after that Dave came walking in. Gary went up to him to see what's going on. "You look like shit too, what happened?"

Dave didn't know what Chris told him, so he didn't know what to say. Dave said, "Chris didn't tell you?"

"He said that he didn't remember anything."

"Nothing happened, we just drank way too much and we passed out at Chris's apartment."

"Good thing I didn't go because at least one of us doesn't look or feel like shit."

Then Dave went over to talk to Chris. He said, "You can't say anything about the women from last night."

"I'm not going to say anything, what did Heather say?"

"She was sleeping, so I put my clothes on and left before she woke up." Dave figured that he would text her in a little bit and tell her what he had told Gary.

When Dave got home from work, Heather was sitting in the living room waiting for him. "I'm sorry about last night. I didn't think I drank that much and all of a sudden it hit me. Then I took Chris home, and was going to take a little nap but ended up sleeping longer than I wanted to. All I could think about was you, and I wanted to come home, but Chris kept talking me into drinking more."

Heather asked, "Who drove?"

"I did."

"Well maybe you should've left his ass there." Then she handed him an envelope.

Dave knew that this wasn't going to be good. It was pictures of him lying in bed with Ashley. Dave didn't know what to say.

Heather said, "Before you lie and say that nothing happened, you left the condom on the end of the bed."

Dave had no choice but to tell her everything that he remembered, which was not much. "We were drinking then I honestly don't remember anything." It still didn't help because he was convinced that he had sex with the woman.

Now Heather was having second-guessing the woman that he cuddled with, lying about having sex with him. "Did you and the other women that you cuddled with, lie before about not having sex?"

"I never lied about the other women. I honestly never had sex with any of them."

"It doesn't matter now, just leave."

Dave grabbed some of his stuff, texted Chris and told him what happened. Then he told Chris that he was going to have to stay there for a little while.

When he got to Chris's apartment, Chris was getting ready to go to an appointment. Chris and Gary never said anything to Dave about the appointment because he had enough going on. They figured they would let him and Heather talk about things. They didn't know how bad things really were. Chris asked, "How did Heather get the pictures and who took them?"

"They were in the mailbox, and I don't know who put them there. There was a condom on the bed so it really doesn't matter."

"You're more than welcome to stay here."

"Oh geez, thanks, since this is your fault anyways."

"My fault? I never told you to keep drinking."

"Actually, yes you did, and I think you called me a little bitch once."

Chris with a confused look asked, "did I? Well I guess it is my fault then, but I never told you to sleep with her and I was drinking so I might have called you a little bitch. I'm very sorry, so what's next? I'd go and tell Heather that it was my fault but that won't work because of the pictures." Chris had to leave for an appointment so he gave Dave his old key back so he could leave if he wanted to.

Dave figured that he would see if Amy wasn't busy and would meet up with him. She wasn't doing anything so she told Dave that they could meet up.

They decided to meet up at the park like they usually did. When Dave got there, Amy wasn't there yet, so he sat on a park bench waiting for her to get there. He wasn't there too long before she got there. When she got there, she sat down next to Dave and asked, "what's going on?

"I messed up really bad and don't think that I can make this one right."

"What did you do?"

"Me and Chris went to the bar and I woke up next to a strange woman then tried to lie to Heather about it so I wouldn't lose her. Then the next day, someone put pictures of us lying next to each other, in our mailbox."

Amy didn't really know what to say this time. "A lot of people make mistakes and some of the times the other person will forgive the person. It may take time, but it could still work out in the end."

"I sure hope so. I'm really going to miss her and really never spent time with Anna."

"I'll help you any way that I can. I told Heather that if you guys ever need a babysitter that I'm more than happy to watch Anna. Maybe you two need a night out alone. "Amy put her arm around Dave and said, "I'm sure everything will work out in the end."

"Thanks, and I really hope it does." They sat there for a little while longer talking and enjoying each other's company until Amy had to leave.

Chris arrived at his appointment and a pretty woman answered the door in a bikini. Chris said, "Hi I'm Chris from Cuddles."

"Come on in, I was just laying out back getting a little sun. Since it's nice out, you don't mind hanging out outside do you?"

"No that's fine."

"Well come on then. How's your day going?"

"It's good." He thought to himself that after seeing her his day just might have gotten better. Then he remembered about his past appointments so he was waiting for this woman to turn crazy. They went out back and sat on her patio furniture not too far from her pool. They were sitting there and having a nice conversation. This was the best appointment that Chris has ever had.

"Me and my boyfriend had broken up and I remembered seeing your fliers so I thought I'd give it a try. I didn't want to spend such a nice day alone."

"No day's good to be alone."

"Yeah I guess you're right."

As they were sitting there a bee started flying around by them. "Shit there's a bee and I'm allergic to them." She said, "I've been seeing a lot of them lately." She got up and went in the house to get the fly swatter. When she came back out, Chris took the fly swatter from her because he didn't want her to get stung. He took it and killed the bee. Then they sat back down and continued talking. The woman said, "Thanks for killing it."

"It's no big deal, we don't need you swelling up." Then another bee started flying around so Chris killed that one too. "Wow I guess you do have a lot of bees around here." Then all of a sudden there were a bunch more bees flying around them.

The woman said, "We can go hang out in the house and I'll call someone in the morning to come take care of the bee problem."

"Don't worry about it, I'll take care of it, it will only take a second." Chris decided to go see where the bees were coming from. He walked around the side of the house and found the nest. It was a pretty big one, but Chris didn't want to be a sissy; plus, he already told the woman that he would take care of it. Chris started to have second thoughts about getting rid of the nest. He asked, "Do you have a ladder, broom and something to put the nest in?"

"I don't have a ladder but I got a broom and will a garbage bag work?"

"Yeah, a garbage bag will work; and here's a bucket that I

can probably stand on."

Then she gave him a broom and a garbage bag to use for the nest. Chris stood on the bucket so that he could take care of the nest, but was a little too short to hit the nest with the broom. The woman said. "Don't worry about it, I'll call someone tomorrow."

Chris said, "No, I got this." He was going to knock the nest in the garbage bag so it wasn't a big deal. As he was trying to knock the nest down with the broom, he lost his balance and the bucket fell over. As Chris was falling, he hit the nest with the broom and it fell on the ground next to him. It looked like a hundred bees started flying around. The woman ran into the house and Chris started waving his hands around to keep the bees from him. There were too many of them, so he took off running around the pool.

The woman yelled, "JUMP IN THE POOL!" Chris heard her yelling, and jumped in the pool. Finally, the bees all flew away and Chris got out of the pool. Then the woman came out and apologized, "I'm sorry, and thanks anyways." Then she handed him his money. She said with an embarrassed smile, "Well, it was fun while it lasted." Chris was standing there dripping wet with a few bee stings and his face was a little swollen. Then she walked him around to the front gate and he left to go home.

CHAPTER 8

When he got back to his apartment, Dave was sitting there watching television. He walked in and sat down next to Dave on the couch. Dave looked at him with a smile and asked, "What happened to you?"

"Well it started with one bee, then another bee, finally a whole lot of bees and she's allergic to bees." Dave looked at Chris with a confused look. "Anyways she was going to call someone in the morning, but I had it." Dave was still really confused. "I stood on the bucket, going to knock the bees' nest in the garbage bag. Then the bucket fell over, and of course I knocked the nest down with the broom. "Bees everywhere, she ran, I ran and I got stung a few times."

By this time, Dave was starting to understand what

happened, but was still confused why Chris was all wet. "Why are you all wet?"

"Oh yeah, she ran in the house and I jumped into the pool."

Dave just smiled and said, "That sucks."

"Yeah it does, how did it go with Amy?"

"We talked and I'm just going to take this one day at a time."

While they were talking, Kim called to tell Dave that they were going to bury Betty in the morning. She said, "They're not going to have a funeral or anything because she didn't have anything set up." She did have a time that they were going to do it so that if anyone wanted to show up, they could.

Dave said, "Thanks, and I'll be there."

The next day, Dave called into work so that he could be there when they buried Betty. She didn't have any family and Dave didn't feel that anyone should be buried alone. When Dave got there, there were only a couple of nurses from the nursing home there. Kim was there and walked up to Dave. She put her hand on his shoulder and said, "Thanks for coming." The chaplain that handles everything at the nursing home was there for a little service. After the little service they said a prayer for Betty and then they lowered the casket. Everyone walked away except for Dave. Kim noticed that Dave was still standing there and walked back to where he was standing. She said, "Betty really never talked too much, but after you left, she talked more than she had in a long time. You really touched her."

"I'm glad that I could help her out. I really didn't know her but I'm sure she was a great woman."

"She was a great woman." Then Dave and Kim walked away so they could leave.

While Dave was at the cemetery, Chris and Gary were working. They were talking about what had happened the night at the club. "I feel bad because Dave kept trying to leave and I wouldn't let him." Chris said, "I guess I kept siding with the women and talking Dave into staying."

Gary said, "Lisa and Heather have been talking about what had happened. Heather said that she misses him, but she can't trust him because he cheated on her. I told Heather that I've known Dave for a long time and he wouldn't cheat on her. I'm positive that he didn't sleep with any of the women that he cuddled with. It's a cuddling business and that's all."

"What did Heather say about all that?"

"She just asked me if I was there, and I told her no. Then she asked me, how do I know that he didn't sleep with any of them, then? Then she immediately asked me if I was so sure, then why was there a condom on the bed? I told her that I just know that he didn't and there has to be an explanation for all this."

Chris replied, "I wish there was an explanation." Then they went and checked the web site and there was a message. Gary figured since Chris went on the last one, that he would go to this one. Plus, Dave had the next day off, so he was going to pick up Anna for the night.

Since Heather didn't have the baby for the night and Gary was going on an appointment, Lisa figured that she would hang out with Heather. When Gary was ready for his appointment, he gave Lisa a hug and kiss then told her that he loved her. Then Gary left for his appointment and Lisa left to go to Heather's house. When Gary got to the woman's house, he went up and knocked on the door. A younger woman that was in her late twenties answered the door. Gary said, "Hi, I'm Gary from Cuddles."

The woman replied, "Come on in and have a seat." They walked over to the couch and sat down. She grabbed her remote and starting going through the channels. There was a movie starting and she asked, "Is this good?"

"It's fine."

"I messaged you because I broke up with my boyfriend and could use some company right now."

"How long have you been broken up for?"

"Since yesterday." Gary was a little confused. "We break up all the time. We'll probably get back together by tomorrow."

Now Gary was really confused. "Then why did you call me over here to cuddle and hang out? You could've had him come over and do it. I believe there's thing called make up sex, I could be wrong but I think that would be a lot more fun than just cuddling."

"I had you come over so that I could make him jealous."

"If you keep getting back together, then why keep breaking up?"

"Because he makes me mad."

"Relationships are not easy, and if you two love each other you can work it out."

"That's the same thing my shrink said." Now Gary started going from confused to being scared. Then all of a sudden, he heard a man banging on the door and yelling, "LET ME IN!"

"I don't know what is going on but is that your ex-boyfriend?"

"Yes, and he's a really jealous person. He must be coming to get his wallet." Then she reached for the wallet on the coffee table and took some money out of it to pay Gary.

Gary said, "Now what?" She replied, "You might want to go out the back door." She took him to the back door so he could leave. Gary walked around the house and waited for her to let him in so he could go to his car.

While Gary was at his appointment, Dave and Chris were hanging out at the apartment. There wasn't much going on for the night because Gary had the only appointment for the night. Dave had his daughter so he couldn't go out anywhere. After what had happened the last time they went out, Dave didn't really care to. Gary stopped by Chris's apartment after he left his appointment since Lisa wasn't going to be home. Chris and Dave asked, "How did your appointment go?"

"I think she was crazy."

Chris replied, "How many women aren't crazy?"

Dave said, "Heather's not crazy, so there's one."

Chris said, "Anyways what happened?"

Gary started to tell them that it started out pretty good. "We were just sitting there watching television and talking. Then she said that she broke up with her boyfriend."

Chris asked, "What's crazy about that, people break up all the time?" Then Chris looked at Dave with an I'm sorry I shouldn't have said that, kind of look.

"Well I told her that if they loved each other they should be able to work out their problems. Then she said that's what her shrink says."

Chris said, "If she sees a shrink, then she's definitely crazy."

Then Gary added, "Oh yeah, her jealous boyfriend came over and started banging on the door, then I had to run out the back door to leave."

Dave and Chris both looked at Gary with a surprised look. Dave asked, "Did you get paid?"

"Yeah, she took it out of his wallet."

Dave said, "His wallet, I thought he was outside banging on the door?"

"He left his wallet there, he was probably banging on the door so he could get it."

Chris said, "She paid a man with her ex-boyfriend's money to come cuddle with her. Yeah she's definitely crazy."

As Gary was sitting there, Lisa texted him to see if he was home and wanted her to pick him up something to eat? He was hungry so he told her yeah, and left so that he would be home when she got there.

The next day, Dave was at the apartment with Anna while Chris and Gary worked. He was just sitting around, playing with the baby and watching television. Then he went and put Anna down for a nap. He sat back down on the couch and continued watching television. He decided to get up and get something to eat. He put something in the microwave to heat it up so he could eat. As it was in the microwave he went and checked the website. There was a message so he read it. Dave thought that since he wasn't working and had to take Anna home later that he would take care of it. Dave texted Chris to tell him about the message and would handle it.

"I know, Gary and I saw it. I'll go if you don't really want to, plus you have Anna."

"I was going to take her home, then go to the appointment."

"That's fine if that's what you want to do."

"I'm good and I need to get out anyways." Then he went to eat his food and start getting ready for his appointment. He figured he would get ready before the baby woke up.

Chris got home from work as Dave was getting the baby ready to take her home. They talked for a few minutes before Dave had to leave. Chris asked, "What time do you have to take Anna home?"

"I'm going to leave here in a minute. How was work?"

"Slow most of the day but it got busy a few times."

As they were talking, Dave texted Heather to tell her that he was getting ready to bring Anna home. She said that she was showing a house and wasn't going be there. Now Dave didn't know what to do. He called Amy to see if she could watch Anna while he went on his appointment. "Hey there, can you watch Anna for a little bit while I go to an appointment?"

"I can't now, I'm doing some running around and won't be home."

"It's no big deal, it was last minute."

"If you would've said something earlier, I could've changed my plans."

"No, it's fine."

"You know I'll watch that beautiful little girl anytime."

"I know, well finish your running and I'll talk to you later." Dave asked Chris, "I can't believe that I'm about to say this, but can you watch Anna?"

Chris looked at Dave like he was crazy. "Me watch the baby?

By the way that was hurtful what you said."

"What did I say?"

Chris sarcastically said, "I can't believe I'm about to say this."

"I'm sorry if I offended you but I have no other choice."

"What about Lisa and Gary?"

"I wouldn't have the time to run over there and make it to the appointment on time. Well then you'll have to go."

"I'm not ready to go anywhere. Give me the baby, how hard can this be?"

"Are you sure?"

"Yes, give me the baby."

Dave handed the baby to Chris and set the diaper bag on the floor. "If there's any problems"

Before Dave could finish, Chris told him, "Go, I got this."

"Are you sure?"

"GO!" Dave took off to his appointment.

When Dave got to the woman's house, he knocked on the door and waited for her to answer. When she answered the door Dave said, "Hi, I'm Dave from Cuddles." She said, "Come on in and thanks for coming. Would you like something to drink?"

"I'm fine."

They walked over to the couch and sat down. The woman snuggled right up to Dave and said, "I could fall asleep right here."

"Not to be nosy, but why did you message us?"

"I just had a baby a few months ago, and while I was pregnant my ex-boyfriend left me."

"That sucks that he left you, and I just had a baby. I'm sorry that you have to go through this because I know how hard it can be to raise a child on your own."

"I have family and friends that help me out a lot."

"That's good that you have them to help you."

"How old is your baby, and are you still with the mom?"

"She's a little over a week and right now I'm not with her mom but I'm hoping we get back together." He didn't tell her what exactly the reason was that they weren't together.

"Do you see her a lot?"

"We just recently broke up, but I had her last night."

"That's good, did you have to take her home before you came here?"

"I was, but her mom was working, so I have my immature childless friend watching her."

"What?"

"Now that I think about it, I probably should have brought her with me."

"Actually, you could've."

"It's no big deal, she'll be fine I hope."

While they were sitting there talking, the baby started to wake up. The woman took a deep breath then said, "Every time I sit down and get comfortable." Dave said, "Don't get up, I got this."

"No, you have your own baby to worry about."

"You need a break, and while I'm here, you can have one."

"She's in the first room on the right."

Dave got up and went to take care of the baby. He took the baby out of her crib and changed her diaper. Then he carried her out into the kitchen and got her bottle out of the fridge. After he got her bottle, he walked into the living room and sat down on the couch to feed her. The woman tried to take the baby from Dave to feed her, but Dave was not going to have that. He insisted, "Relax!" She decided to just let Dave go because he wasn't going to give in. Finally, the baby fell back to sleep so Dave took her and put her back in her crib. Then he walked back out into the living room and continued cuddling with the woman.

"Thanks, and you didn't have to do that."

"I know, but I wanted to." When the time was up, the woman went to get money to pay Dave. Dave told her, "Don't worry about it, you're a single mom and have a baby to take care of."

"I'm a registered nurse and I'm not hurting for money, we'll be fine. So, here, take this." She held out her hand with the money in it.

"I'll take the money, but I'm not going to accept a tip." The woman looked at him with a smile and said, "What tip? I'm going to tip you and you're going to keep it. After everything you did, you deserve it."

Dave paused for a minute, shook his head, smiled, and took the money.

Then she gave him a hug, a kiss on the cheek and said, "I hope everything works out for you with you and your ex. You're a great guy, I'm sure everything will work out for you in the end."

Dave replied, "Thanks."

Then she walked Dave to the door so he could leave.

As Dave was at his appointment, Chris was watching Anna. Dave told Chris that the she was fed and had a clean diaper, but that didn't last for long. Anna started crying then Chris just closed his eyes, shook his head and took a deep breath. He didn't know what to do so he picked her up and held her to see if she would quit crying. She kept crying so he grabbed his phone and looked up reasons that she might be crying. Some of the reasons were because they could be hungry, tired, need their diaper changed, ate too much, etc. Chris figured that she wasn't tired, because she just woke up. He picked her up to smell her diaper and that didn't smell like she needed it changed. He didn't think that she ate too much, because she hadn't eaten in a little while, and just woke up. The only thing he could think of is that she was hungry again. He put her down and went into the kitchen to get her bottle. He put it in the microwave to heat it up. When the timer went off, he opened the door to take the bottle out, but he put it in too long. He yelled and dropped the bottle on the floor because it was too hot. He grabbed a towel to pick the bottle up and threw it in the freezer to cool it off. He even threw the towel in there with the bottle. After a few minutes, he took the bottle out of the freezer and went back into the living room to feed Anna.

After she was done drinking her bottle, he picked her up to burp her. Then he started to smell something. Once again Chris closed his eyes, shook his head and took a deep breath. He never changed a diaper before so he didn't know what he was doing. He figured that when he took it off, he would do the complete opposite to put the clean one on. When he started to take the dirty one off, the smell got worse. He said to himself, "Oh man, I think I'm going to puke. This is disgusting, I don't know why people have babies." As he was changing the diaper, he used way too many baby wipes and had a look of disgust on his face. After he was done wiping her clean, he went to finish putting the diaper on and she started to pee. With a look of disgust, he said, "Really you couldn't have done this earlier when you pooped?" He grabbed a bunch more baby wipes and started to wipe her again. Then he took the wet diaper and threw it on the pile of baby wipes. Once again, he got out a clean diaper and put it on Anna.

Chris put the baby down so that he could clean up the mess on the floor. Instead of just picking the mess up with his hands, he got the broom, dustpan, and wastebasket. Then he used the broom to sweep up the baby wipes and dirty diapers into the dustpan. Then he emptied the dustpan into the wastebasket. He took the wastebasket back into the kitchen. The garbage was stinking up his apartment, so he went and got the spray out of his bathroom. He started spraying all over his apartment; he even sprayed the inside and outside of the wastebasket. He used the whole can of spray and when he was done, he threw the empty can in the garbage. Then he went in to the living room and waited for Dave to get back. By this time Anna was sleeping, so Chris sat down to watch television.

Shortly after he sat down, Dave walked in and started sniffing the air. "How was Anna? I hope she wasn't a problem."

"No, she was fine, she slept most of the time. She woke up and was hungry so I gave her a bottle."

"I didn't think that she would be hungry again this early."

"Then she needed her diaper changed so I changed it."

Dave was surprised that he changed a diaper. "I'm sorry about that."

"Oh yeah by the way, you're going to need more baby wipes. Oh, and can you pick up some more spray for the bathroom?"

Dave thought to himself that there were a lot of baby wipes and a new can of spray in the bathroom. He walked over to the garbage and opened it. When he opened it, he realized why he needed more baby wipes and a can of spray. After seeing that, Dave was shocked that he didn't need to buy more diapers. Chris asked, "Oh yeah can you take the garbage out when you leave?"

"Yeah, I'll take care of it." Then he took the garbage bag out, tied it up, and put an empty bag in the wastebasket. Dave took the garbage out, then he left to take Anna home because he had to work in the morning.

CHAPTER 9

The next day, there were three messages on the website, so after work all three of them ran home to get ready to go. Chris's appointment was the earliest, so he had to leave first. When he got there, the address was a motel. He thought that he must have written it down wrong or something. It had a room number so he figured it was an apartment. He thought that he would go to the room number that he had written down to see if there was someone expecting him. Chris went to the room and knocked on the door. A beautiful woman answered the door then Chris asked, "I'm Chris from Cuddles, did you message me to come here?"

"Yes, I did, come on in." She looked a little familiar, but Chris wasn't sure where he would have known her from. They walked over to the bed and sat down. Chris thought it was weird that she had him come to a motel. He thought maybe she was married, in a relationship, or wanted sex. "If you messaged me to come over and have sex, I can't do that, the business is just for cuddling and that is all."

As they were talking, a little person walked into the room. Chris instantly stopped and looked at the man and said, "I didn't know. I just got a message and came to the address that she gave me."

The man insisted, "Shut up!"

Chris looked at the woman and she whispered, "Sorry."

The man said, "I'm her pimp and you owe me $300."

"Excuse me? She messaged me and if anyone owes anyone, she owes me. So, I'm not paying nothing and there's nothing you can do about it."

"You're right, I can't do anything about it, but he can." Then he pointed behind Chris.

"Let me guess, there's a big scary man behind me." Chris turned slowly around, scared and confused, to look behind himself. Chris was right, there was a big scary man standing there looking at him. Chris turned back to the other man, got out his wallet and started going through his money. He looked at the man and said, "All I have is $75 and a gift card to the Mexican restaurant up the road."

"Good enough."

Chris handed him the money and gift card then walked

away. As he was leaving, he said, "This really isn't a good way to run a business, you'll never get returning customers this way." Then the big guy took a step towards Chris and he walked faster out of the room.

Chris hurried up to get to his car so that he could leave. He got to his apartment and Dave was getting ready for his appointment. Dave asked, "What are you doing back already?"

Chris told him what had happened. "I went to the appointment and it was at a motel. I went to the door, a beautiful woman answered and then her pimp came in then robbed me."

Dave with a confused look replied, "What?"

"What part of beautiful woman and got robbed don't you understand?"

"Did you know her?"

"No Dave, I don't run around getting prostitutes."

"I don't know what you do since I moved out."

"Well, I don't get prostitutes, plus I got the internet."

"I'm not even going to ask what that means."

"Yeah it's probably better that you don't. Wait a minute, it was one of the women from the club the other night."

"Are you sure?"

"Yeah I'm pretty sure."

As they were talking, Gary called Dave and said, "I must have written the address down wrong, because the one I have is at a motel."

Dave looked at Chris and told Gary, "Leave, get out of there as fast as you can."

Gary was confused and asked, "What, Why?"

"Just go, and come over here, then I'll explain."

"Alright whatever." Then the two of them hung up their phones.

Dave told Chris, "Gary's appointment was at a motel too."

Chris asked, "What's going on?"

"You know more than me. When Gary gets here, we'll see if we can figure out what's going on."

Gary was confused but thought he would do what Dave said and leave. As he was getting ready to leave, the pimp's bodyguard stood behind his car so he couldn't go anywhere. The man was pretty big, so Gary didn't say anything. Then there was a knock on the window and a little person was standing there. He asked, "Are you from the cuddle place?"

Gary nervously answered, "Yes."

"That's good because you owe me $500."

Why would I owe you $500?"

The pimp looked at Gary, pointed at the big guy and said, "Because he said so."

Gary was scared, so he grabbed the money out of his wallet and gave it to the pimp. The pimp looked in shock that Gary had $500 on him. The pimp said, "Thanks." Then his bodyguard moved aside so that Gary could leave.

Gary pulled over a little way up the road to call Dave to tell him what had happened. "I just got robbed."

"Shit, ok just get over here."

Chris and Dave went to the computer to look up the appointments and all three were at motels. Dave and Chris looked at each other with a confused look. Of course, Dave didn't go to his appointment.

When Dave got off the phone with Gary, he asked Chris, "What's going on?"

"Are we just going to beat this to death because I already said I don't know. All I know is that we had to have been set up. If it was the woman from the club, then you were probably set up that night at the club."

"I wish it was that easy, but there was a condom on the bed, so it's not going to matter anyways."

Chris mentioned, "I wonder if one of us said something about the cuddling business at the club, then the women went back and told their pimp."

"I don't know because someone kept me there all night drinking and I don't remember too much."

"Yeah that's my bad and next time we're definitely leaving earlier."

"Really, next time?"

"Well, you are single now."

"Whatever, I'm just going to sit here, watch television and see if I can figure out what can be going on."

As they were sitting there, Gary came walking in and asked, "What's"

Before he could get it all out Chris cautioned, "If you say that I swear I'm going to punch you in your face."

Dave said, "Calm down. We don't know what 's going on and we've been trying to figure it out."

Chris told Gary, "I think the woman that was in the room when they got me was one of the women from the club."

Gary asked, "Why would they rob me?"

Dave got ready to say something then Chris interrupted him. "I think I figured it out." Dave and Gary just looked at him to see what he had to say. "She was really into me and her pimp didn't like it. She went to meet me at the motel so he wouldn't know, and he followed her there."

Dave said, "Yeah that's probably it."

"What about Heather's ex-boyfriend?" Gary asked, "He set you up before."

"That would make sense, but I don't think he has anything to do with it. Heather hasn't heard from him or seen him since she hit him and told him to stay away."

They couldn't figure anything out, so Gary decided to go home. When he got home, he told Lisa about what had happened. "Me and Chris got robbed by a pimp today."

"Why would a pimp want to rob you? You guys have a cuddling business and that has nothing to do with sex, unless he thinks that you guys are having sex with your clients."

"That still doesn't make sense, because we would be having sex with women and he has women having sex with men."

"Well you never know, maybe his women are having sex with other women."

"Yeah because there were the two women that beat Chris up. I think it might have something to do with Heather's ex-boyfriend, but Dave doesn't think so."

"I'll call my brother and see if he can find anything out."

"I'm not judging or anything, but does your brother get prostitutes?"

"No, but he knows a lot of people and maybe someone knows something, so it won't hurt to talk to him. Plus, he's very protective over me, and you're my husband, so he won't be very happy about it."

"If you think it will work."

"He might bust your balls and say that you need to grow a pair" Then she smiled and said, "By the way, I like your balls." Then she kissed him.

The next day at work, Gary went up to Dave and Chris to tell him about what Lisa said. He mentioned that she thought it might be because the pimp's women are having sex with other women so he's mad about the cuddling business. Gary said, "Remember the two women that beat up Chris?"

"I didn't get beat up by two women, I accidently got in the way of one of the women trying to hit the other woman."

"You got hit and knocked out." Dave said, "In my book you got beat up," Then Dave and Gary smiled then hi fived each other.

"Whatever, me getting hit had nothing to do with this, we need to focus on what just happened."

Gary said, "Lisa talked to her brother to see if he could find something out."

Chris asked, "Why, does her brother get prostitutes?"

"No, I thought the same thing, but she did say that he will probably say I have a vagina or something."

Chris said, "Me and Dave have been thinking that for a long time."

Dave said, "don't listen to him, we still have a business to run and we'll have to be very careful. Then we'll see if Lisa's brother can find something out."

Later that night, they had an appointment, but Gary had plans with his wife and Dave was going to pick up Anna then meet up with Amy. So, Chris was going to have to go on the appointment.

He actually didn't mind this one because it was at a movie theater, so he felt safe. The woman asked if someone would meet her there because she wanted to see a movie but didn't want to watch it by herself. Chris was getting ready to go and then he went into the living room with a confused look on his face to talk to Dave. He asked, "How is this supposed to work?" He didn't know if it was like a date and he was supposed to pay, or if she was supposed to pay.

"I don't know, just plan on paying for yourself and her paying for herself. She probably just wants someone to cuddle with while watching a movie."

"How am I supposed to charge her?"

"You'll have to figure it out when you get there."

"I'll figure something out." Then he started to walk back to his room to finish getting ready. He stopped and went back into the living room. "Oh yeah, can I borrow some money? That pimp took all my money, my gift card, and I haven't gone to the bank yet."

"Don't you have a debit card?"

"Yeah I do have a debit card but I don't know if I have any money in my account." Dave shook his head and handed Chris some money. Chris said, "That's why I haven't gone to the bank." After Dave handed Chris some money, he left to pick up Anna and meet up with Amy. Then Chris finished getting ready so he could go on his appointment.

Chris got to the movie theater and there was a woman

standing out front. He asked, “Are you Becky?”

“Yes, and you must be from Cuddles.”

“Yes, and I’m Chris.”

She was there waiting for him and already had bought the tickets. “I already got the tickets and everything is on me.”

Chris felt bad and said, “Since you got the tickets, let me get the food and drinks.”

“I asked you to come, so I’ll pay.”

Chris insisted, “I’m going to get the food and drinks.”

She finally agreed, “Alright then.” Then they walked up to the concession stand to get their stuff.

After Chris bought the food and drinks, they went to head over to the theater that the movie was showing in. As he turned around to walk away, some kids went running by and knocked the stuff in his hands all over him. Chris got ready to say something but their dad was standing there so he just kept to himself. Then he turned back around to the counter and told the girl, “Hey some kids knocked all my stuff all over.”

She said, “I can see that because it’s all over you, do you want more?”

“Well yeah.” She got his popcorn, drinks and told him how much money he owed her. He got his wallet out but didn’t have enough money. He had already spent the money that Dave had loaned him. He asked Becky, “Hey can I get some money?” He started rambling, "I got robbed, got gas on my way here and my bank account is a little short this week so I can't use my debit card."

Becky had a confused look on her face as she said, "Don't worry about it." She handed him some money and said, "I owe you money anyways. Let me know how much more that I owe you."

"You don't owe me anything else, this is fine." Then they went to watch the movie.

When the movie was over, Chris walked Becky to her car. She gave Chris a hug and said, "Thanks for watching a movie with me."

"No problem."

"I just didn't want to watch a movie by myself."

"It's no problem and thanks for inviting me." Then he walked to his car and headed home.

Dave picked up Anna and took her to the park to meet up with Amy. When Dave got there Amy was already there. Amy excitingly said, "There's my baby girl." Then Dave handed Anna to her. Amy asked Dave, "How have you been?"

"Not bad, could be better."

"Have you and Heather talked about stuff yet?"

"Not really, just about Anna."

"I thought things would start to blow over by now."

"It would be nice but I really messed up this time. Oh yeah, Chris and Gary got robbed."

"Robbed?"

"They went on appointments and I guess a pimp robbed them."

"Why would a pimp rob them?"

"We don't know, but we think it had something to do with the women at the club, because Chris went to an appointment at a motel and the woman that was there, he thought was one of the women from the club."

"First off, if someone's messaging you to go to a motel, it's either they probably want sex, or they're probably hiding something. Did you guys say anything to them about the business?"

"I don't remember."

"How much did you drink that night?" Dave answered, "I don't think it was any more than I normally do."

"Apparently something happened or was said that night. Why would a pimp or prostitutes do something like this?"

"All I remember was sitting there drinking then every time that I would want to leave, the women talked me into drinking another beer."

"So, they wouldn't let you leave and wanted you to keep drinking?"

"Yes."

"It sounds like you were set up. If you drank like you usually do and this never happened, then you were probably drugged. It only takes a second to put something in someone's drink."

"We never thought about that."

"Have you ever felt like this in the morning after you were drinking?"

Not since I was a teenager, plus I was driving so I would never intentionally get that drunk."

"That's what it sounds like to me, you were set up and drugged."

"It makes sense, but I do remember Chris drinking a lot more than he normally does."

Amy joked, "Well, Chris will get shit faced at a kids birthday party."

"That's true. I love Heather and would never knowingly cheat on her. If I just had proof then I could hopefully make things right with Heather."

CHAPTER 10

Gary and Lisa went shopping then to get something to eat. Then they decided it was a nice day, so they went for a little walk and to get some ice cream. As they were walking Gary stopped and urged Lisa, "We should probably turn around and head back."

"Why? We're having a nice time."

Well, I got to work in the morning and just think we should head back."

Lisa knew that something was wrong so she asked, "What's going on?"

"It's nothing, let's just head back."

Lisa knew that there was something wrong. She said, "I'm not going anywhere until you tell me what's wrong and why you want to go home."

Then he broke down and told Lisa what the problem was. He said, "Those guys up there are the ones that robbed me." Then he pointed at two men and two women. Gary didn't want to walk past them.

"That's the guy that robbed you?"

"Yeah and let's just go."

Lisa thought it might be a good idea to turn around. They turned around, took a few steps and Lisa stopped to look back at those guys.

Gary asked, "Is there something wrong?"

Lisa said, "No, let's go." Then they walked back to their car and left to go home.

The next day at work, Dave told Chris and Gary, "Amy thinks that we were set up and I was drugged."

Chris asked, "Drugged, we were drugged?"

"I don't know if you were drugged or not, but we think I was."

Chris sighed, "Good, because I don't need to become addicted to drugs."

Gary said, "You won't get addicted if you do them one time."

"How do you know, are you a drug expert?"

"No, but I'm pretty sure that you can't."

Then Chris looked at Dave and said, "If you were drugged, I'm going to help you through your addiction."

Dave sarcastically asked, "What would I do without you?"

"That's what friends; wait a minute you're being sarcastic aren't you." Dave just shook his head.

Gary asked, "Well this makes sense, but can we prove it to Heather? Can you go to the hospital and get tested?"

"I wish but it's probably too late for that." Dave really wanted to find out if he was drugged, because he wanted Heather back really bad. He knew that might be the only thing he could do to work things out with Heather.

Chris said, "All we can do is keep trying to figure something out so things can go back to the way it was." The three of them continued their day trying to find an answer. They still had a business to run so they periodically checked the website. Then all of a sudden, they had three messages. The funny thing was all three were at the same address and the same time. Something didn't seem right about that, so they agreed that they wouldn't go. They didn't want to get robbed or have something worse happen to them. All they could think about was that it was that pimp trying to set them up again.

That afternoon, Dave and Chris walked into the apartment. They checked the computer and there were three more messages from the address from earlier in the day. The two of them were wondering what was going on here.

Gary also checked the computer when he got home. Gary called Dave and said, "We have more messages from the address from earlier."

"Yeah we just saw that."

"What should we do?"

"I don't know because we are obviously being set up. Well, we can drive by and if things seem sketchy, then we keep driving."

"What if they chase us?"

Dave replied, "I guess we'll have to hope that they don't." Dave told Gary, "Get ready, and we'll be over to pick you up in a little bit."

Gary said, "OK," and hung up the phone so he could get ready. After he hung up with Dave, he tried to call Lisa to tell her about the appointments. Lisa didn't answer, so he left a voicemail with the address and told her what was going on. "We have three messages and they are all at the same address and it seems really weird. So, we're going to drive by and see what's going on and if it doesn't seem right then we're going to keep driving. So, if something happens and I don't make it back, I love you." Then as he was getting ready to hang up, he said, "Oh I'm going to text you the address so if you don't hear from any of us you can give it to the police, IRS or the National Guard." Gary ended up getting ready and waited for Dave and Chris to pick him up.

Dave and Chris finally got there to pick up Gary, then they drove to the address that was on the message. When Gary got in the car there was a baseball bat in the back seat. Gary asked, "What's this for?"

Chris replied, "Well if there trouble it's always good to have a weapon."

"What if they have guns?" Gary asked, "A baseball bat isn't going to be any help against guns."

"OK, maybe I didn't think this through." Chris said, "Yeah but if they don't have guns then you're going to wish that you had a bat." When they got to the address Lisa was sitting on the porch. Chris asked Gary, "What is Lisa doing on the porch?"

"I don't know."

Chris asked, "Why would she want to cuddle with all of us?"

Dave replied, "She's not here to cuddle."

Chris sarcastically asked, "Then why is she here?"

Dave replied, "I don't know, but we're about to find out."

"Do you think that's a good idea?" He asked, "Maybe she's a double agent and she set us up in the first place."

Gary replied, "She's not a double agent."

Chris asked, "How do you know, it happens in the movies all the time?" Now Gary was starting to question if Lisa was a double agent. Then Chris said, "Maybe they kidnaped her to make sure that we come to rescue her."

Dave said, "She's not a double agent, she wasn't kidnapped, and I'm turning around to go back there."

Chris said, "OK but when we're tied up and being tortured,

don't say I didn't warn you."

Dave stopped the car and they walked up to the porch to see what was going on. Gary asked Lisa, "What are you doing here and why are you not answering your phone?"

She replied, "You'll see in a few minutes."

Then Gary asked Lisa, "Are you a double agent?"

"What?" Lisa asked, "Oh by the way the IRS is only going to come look for you if you owe them money, I think you meant the FBI."

Gary answered, "I was nervous when I was leaving the message." The three of them were really confused but they just waited to see what Lisa was talking about.

After about five minutes a car pulled up and parked in front of the house. The pimp, his bodyguard, Ashley, and Tori got out of the car. Dave, Chris and Gary saw them get out of the car, then freaked out. Chris asked, "What the hell Lisa, are you trying to get us killed?"

Gary said to Chris, "Your bat isn't going to do us any good in the car."

Chris said, "See I told you she's a double agent."

Lisa said, "Don't worry about it, I got this."

"Why did you guys call us to meet you here?" The pimp asked, "Do you got some more money for me or are you going to beat me up?" Then the pimp and his bodyguard laughed.

"We didn't call you." Dave said, "We were told to come here." Then all of a sudden, a bunch of motorcycles pulled up. It was Lisa's brother and some of his club members. The pimp and his bodyguard got a scared and confused look on their faces.

Lisa's brother walked up to the pimp and said, "I don't appreciate you messing with my family and their friends. That was my brother in law and my sister that you robbed."

The pimp said, "I never robbed your sister."

Lisa's brother replied, "You robbed her husband, and that's taking money from her too. I think you owe them some money and an apology."

The pimp pulled some money out and handed it to Lisa's brother. He walked up to Gary and asked him how much money he took from him? Gary told him that he took $500.

Chris said, "Wait a minute, you took $500 from him and $300 from me?"

Everyone looked at Chris with a confused look.

"What don't you think I could afford $500?"

Dave shook his head, grabbed Chris and motioned for him to shut up. Dave said, "Plus you only had $75, so no, you couldn't afford $500."

Chris replied, "I guess you got a point."

Dave asked Gary, "Why would you have $500 in your wallet?"

Then Lisa asked, "Yeah why would you?"

"Well just in case I need gas or something."

Then Lisa's brother gave Gary his $500 back. Then he walked up to Chris and said apparently, he took $300 from you, so he handed him $300. Chris said, "Hold on he wanted $300 but I only had $75." Chris got his wallet out and started going through his money. He handed Lisa's brother the $225 that wasn't his money and said, "Here you can give this back."

Lisa's brother shook his head and looked at Chris like he was an idiot. Then he took the money that Chris gave him and stuck it in his pocket.

Chris looked at him and said, "Or you can just keep it." Then Chris started to walk away but turned back around to talk to Lisa's brother. "What about my gift card? I had a gift card for the Mexican restaurant across town but it's ok if he doesn't have it."

Lisa's brother shook his head and looked at the pimp. The pimp took the gift card out of his wallet and handed it to Lisa's brother. Lisa's brother handed it to Chris. The pimp said, "I used it once so I don't know how much money is left on the card."

Chris said, "Oh yeah, have you ate there before?"

"No, that was the first time." "

"It's pretty good, what did you get? They have really good burritos."

"I just got some tacos."

"You should really try the burritos."

Everyone was looking at those two, shaking their heads with confused looks. Then Lisa's brother asked Chris, "Are you done, or do you need more time to plan your date?"

Chris looked at the pimp and replied, "Yeah, I think we're done."

Lisa's brother told the pimp, "I better not hear about you messing with any of these guys or the business again."

Dave asked the pimp, "Were we drugged at the club, and why did you do this?"

"Yes, you were drugged and I was paid to set you up."

Chris said, "That's good, now we can tell Heather that we were drugged and everything can go back to normal."

The pimp looked at Chris and said, "He was drugged, you weren't."

Ashley said, "You drink like a girl so we didn't have to drug you."

"Someone paid us to set you up because you were dating his ex-girlfriend. Then he told me about the cuddling business and a way that we could rob you so I could make money."

Dave asked, "Is his name Jason?"

"Yes it is."

Lisa's brother asked the pimp, "Do you know him?"

"No I don't, he came up to me and talked to me about

setting someone up."

Lisa's brother said, "Then you probably don't know how to get ahold of him then."

"I have his address. I made him give it to me so if something went wrong then I knew where to find him."

Lisa's brother said, "That's good, I'll take that address."

Lisa walked up to her brother and said, "I got an idea. Go get Jason and take him to Heather's so he can tell her what he did. This way Dave will be in the clear." Her brother agreed and got Heathers address from Dave. Then she called Heather and told her that they were coming over.

When they got to Heather's, she came outside to see what they wanted. Lisa said, "Jason paid the pimp to drug Dave then set him up and rob them."

Heather didn't know what to believe. She figured that Lisa wouldn't lie to her. Dave said, "See, I knew there was something wrong, because I love you and would never cheat on you."

"But I still have it in the back of my mind that you slept with another woman."

"I was drugged and didn't know what I was doing."

Chris said, "At least he wore a condom."

Everyone just looked at Chris and shook their heads. Then Dave said to Chris, "Yeah, I know you're just trying to help, but I don't think that's going to work."

As they were talking Lisa's brother and his club members pulled up on their motorcycles. Jason was on the back of one of the motorcycles. Lisa's brother made him go up and tell Heather what he did. Jason walked up to the house and told her about setting those guys up. "Yeah I paid them to set him up because I love you and want you back."

Heather started yelling at Jason, "YOU GOT HIM DRUGGED AND MADE HIM HAVE SEX WITH ANOTHER WOMAN!"

"He didn't have sex with another woman."

"What about the pictures and the condom on the bed?"

"That was from me."

Dave said, "Wait a minute."

Then Chris asked, "Are you saying that Dave had sex with you?"

"Yeah, did I have sex with you?"

"No, you didn't have sex with me."

"Did you have sex with me?"

"No one had sex."

Heather asked, "What about the condom?"

Jason said, "I masturbated in it."

Dave asked, "So nobody had sex?"

Then Chris said, "Apparently Jason's hand had sex."

Gary asked, "If you paid a prostitute to set up someone, why didn't you just have sex with her? You chose to jerk off instead?"

Jason got really embarrassed and said, “Well I guess I didn’t think that through.”

Heather told Jason, “We are done and we are never going to get back together, so stay away from us.”

Lisa’s brother looked at Jason and said, “You heard the woman, and better hope that I don’t have to go looking for you again.”

Then Lisa’s brother and club members got on their motorcycles to leave. Jason ran up to them and asked, “Are you taking me home?”

Lisa’s brother said, “No.”

“How am I getting home?”

“It’s not my problem.”

Jason turned around and looked at everyone else. They all looked at each other and walked in the house.

Later that night, Dave called Amy and told her about what had happened. “You were right; I was drugged and set up.”

“I’m glad that you found out and everything is alright. If you guys want to go out, I’ll watch Anna.”

“We’re good.”

“I wasn’t asking; I want to spend time with Anna. Now get ready to go out and bring her over here.”

Lisa and Gary took Chris home so that he could get ready, then they went home to get ready. When Lisa and Gary were ready, they were going to go pick up Chris so he could ride with them. Lisa and Dave were taking Anna to Amy's, then they were going to meet up with everyone else. They decided that they were going to go get something to eat and go out for some drinks.

After they got done eating, they went to the club for some drinks. They were hanging around at their normal spot by the bar. Then a woman walked up behind Chris. When he turned around, it was Tori from the motel. He jumped and freaked out. He said, "Are you here to drug me and rob me?"

"No, I want to apologize." Then she asked, "I have to go to the restroom, can I come back and talk?"

"That's fine as long as you're not doing anything to me."

As she was walking away everyone was looking at Chris.

"What?" Then someone walked up behind Chris. He thought that it was Tori so he turned around to talk to her. When he turned around, he yelled, "WHAT THE HELL?" It was Lucy; the transgender man or ugly woman from before.

Everyone else giggled and turned their heads the other way. "I missed you and was thinking about making another appointment. I also saw you drive by my house."

"I never drove by your house."

Lucy sarcastically said, "Uh huh."

"What's that supposed to mean?"

"You know." As Lucy was taking to Chris, Tori came walking

up. Lucy said, "Can I help you?"

Tori said, "I can leave if I'm interrupting something?"

Chris said, "No trust me, you're not interrupting anything." As they were standing there everyone else was talking about the cuddling business.

Dave said to Chris, "The women want to bet us."

"About what?"

"They think that they could make more money cuddling in a month than we can."

"It wouldn't be fair because there are three of us and two of them."

Heather said, "Don't worry we'll find someone."

Lucy said, "I'll do it."

Then Heather looked at Tori and said, "Hey new girl, are you looking to make some extra money?"

Once again Lucy said, "I'll do it."

Tori said, "Well as a matter of fact, as of today I'm looking for a job."

Then Lucy said, "If she can't do it, I can."

Everyone was ignoring Lucy. Tori said, "I'm in."

Lucy said to Chris, "I think they were intimidated by my good looks."

Chris replied, "Yeah, that's it."

Tori walked over by everyone else and apologized then she

introduced herself to them. She said, "I'm Tori and I'm sorry about everything you guys went through."

Heather replied, "It's all good now."

Tori said to Lisa, "Tell your brother thanks, I've been trying to find a way out for a long time. Then when your brother said that stuff to him, I told him I was out and if he didn't like it, I was going to find your brother. Then he let me go."

Lisa smiled and said, "If you have any problems, let me know and I'll talk to my brother."

Dave looked around at everyone and said, "Looks like we have a bet." Then he gave Heather a big hug and kiss. Gary gave Lisa a hug and kiss. Chris and Tori looked at each other and Chris held out his hand, then Tori shook it.

-CUDDLES-

VOLUME 3

CHAPTER 11

The next day Dave, Chris and Gary had to work. The women were going to work on the new flyers for the cuddling business, now that they were going to be a part of it. When Gary got off work, he was going to change the website to specify that Cuddles now had women working for them. Chris said, "I can't believe that you two are letting your wife and girlfriend do this."

Gary asked, "Why?"

Chris said, "You know how men are, they're pushy and always horny."

Dave replied, "That's not true, I'm not always pushy or horny."

Gary said, "I'm not, either."

Then Dave said to Gary, "It's just the men not getting any

that are always horny."

Dave and Gary smiled and they hi fived each other. "Oh yeah, what's that supposed to mean?" Chris asked, "OK, never mind, I know exactly what it means."

"We trust them, why wouldn't we?" Dave said, "It'll be fun, plus we have a little friendly bet. It also gives you a chance to bond with Tori."

Chris tried to play it off about Tori and said, "What does that mean, did she say something?"

"No, but we can tell that you like her."

"I was just being nice, the woman tried to ruin your life and our business."

"She was put up to it and probably had no choice. I don't know what the big deal is; she's a very pretty woman."

"I'm just going to watch my back because we don't know if she and her pimp are planning anything again."

"That's fair, but I think after what Lisa's brother said, we're good. The five of us can keep going out and we can have two on one bill, two on another bill, and then you."

"Oh yeah, I'm a fifth wheel because I'm single, how about you get me a booster seat because I'm short."

"I didn't mean anything by it. I think that she likes you and you like her, just give it a chance."

Later that night, Gary was going to fix the website; Dave was going with Heather to hang out with Amy; and Chris was just going to sit home. When Chris got home, he checked the computer for messages since he had no plans. There was a message, so he messaged back saying, "Hey this is Chris, and I'm free tonight anytime." Chris started getting ready just in case he had to go on the appointment.

After a little while, the woman replied back and said, "Anytime is fine."

Chris called Dave to tell them about the message and said, "There's a message so since you guys are busy, I'll go."

"OK, stop by the park when you get done because Gary, Lisa, and Tori are going to be here."

"Oh really, those three just decided that they were going to go to the park."

"As a matter of fact, they did."

"So, were you going to ask me?"

"Actually, I was." Then after a quick pause said, "I was just getting ready to."

"I bet you were."

"Are you coming or not?"

Chris figured that he wasn't doing anything, so he told Dave, "Let me check my schedule." Before he could finish and tell Dave that he would stop out, Dave hung up on him. Then Chris said to himself, "He must be in a bad area because he dropped my call."

After Dave hung up on him, he called Gary to tell him that he was going on the appointment. "There was a message and since you were going to be busy, I'll go." Gary replied, "Yeah I saw that and was going to see if you could go."

"Really when were you going to ask me? Never mind I'm not getting into this with you."

Gary was confused and said, "OK."

"Oh, when I talked to Dave earlier, he must have been going through a tunnel or something because he dropped my call. Can you tell him that I'll come out to the park when I'm done?"

Once again, Gary was confused and replied, "Um yeah." Then they hung up and Gary said to himself, "Tunnel?"

Chris got ready and headed over to the woman's house.

When Chris arrived at the woman's house, he walked up and knocked on the door. The woman answered the door and Chris said, "Hi, I'm Chris from Cuddles."

"Come on in and have a seat but you'll have to take off your shoes because I'm kind of a neat freak."

"It's no problem." After Chris took off his shoes, he realized that he had a hole in one of his socks. He tried to hide it so the woman wouldn't see it.

The woman asked, "Would you like something to drink?"

Chris answered, "Sure."

When she was talking to Chris, he was moving his foot

around to try to fix his sock so that she might not see the hole. "I have pop, tea or water, is there a problem?"

"Um no, no problem and I'll take some water." He kept moving his foot around while he was talking.

Once again with a puzzled look the woman asked, "Are you sure there no problem?"

"Problem? Yes, I have a hole in my sock and was trying to fix it so you wouldn't see it."

"It's just a hole."

"Yeah my dog must have gotten ahold of it."

"Have a seat and I'll be right back."

Chris said to himself, "Dog, I don't even have a dog, why did I even say that?"

Then he sat down on the couch while the woman was in the kitchen getting their drinks. When he sat down, he started trying to fix his sock again. When she got their drinks, she came back into the living room and handed Chris his glass of water. Then she sat down on the couch and cuddled up next to him. Then she asked, "Have you ever did more than just cuddle?"

Chris wasn't thinking about what she meant and replied, "No, what else would we do?" Then Chris picked up his glass of water and took a drink.

While he was taking a drink she replied, "You know, sex."

Chris immediately spit out the drink of water. "Excuse me?

I'm sorry about that because I was going to start choking and spit it out before I did."

"No problem, it will dry up. So, have you ever had sex when you went to cuddle with someone?"

"No, because it's a cuddling business." The woman started kissing on Chris's neck and he started to get really nervous. He moved his head away and said, "Ok, so you are very friendly but let's be friendly in a cuddling way." The woman laid her head on Chris's shoulder. "See this is nice, cuddling, watching television and talking, so what made you message us anyways?"

"I'm horny." Then she started nibbling on Chris's ear.

Chris pulled his head away again and said, "Did you say that you're hungry, because if you are, I can go get you something to eat?" Then he started to stand up and pointed then said. "Is that the kitchen over there?"

The woman pulled him back down on the couch and said, "Ok, I'll behave but you don't know what you're missing."

Chris nervously tried to change the subject. He pointed at the television and said, "I am missing something, how did this guy end up in jail?" The woman then snuggled up next to Chris and started rubbing his leg.

He pushed her hand off of his leg and got ready to say something, but the woman shushed him then jumped on his lap. As she was getting on top of him, she looked out the window and saw that her husband was pulling in the driveway. She jumped up and exclaimed, "You have to go!"

Chris nervously asked, "Go where?"

"My husband's home and you have to get out."

Chris got ready to run to the front door, and the woman stopped him. She said, "He will see you leaving, you have to go out the bedroom window." Chris started to run towards the bedroom then the woman grabbed him. She reached in her bra, grabbed some money and handed it to him. Chris grabbed it with a look of disgust on his face because it was all wet from the woman's sweat between her breasts. Then she grabbed him again and kissed him on his lips and said, "Now get out!"

Chris ran in the bedroom, opened the window and climbed out it. As he was climbing out of it, he fell into the bushes. Chris climbed out of the bushes and stepped into a pile of dog poop. Then with a look of disgust he said, "Really, figures they would have a dog." Then he looked up and thought about what he said to himself about the dog. As he looked up, he started to hear a growl. He looked over and there was the dog growling at him. Chris said, "Shit." Then he took off running toward the fence. The dog started to run after him, but he made it over the fence before the dog could catch up to him. When he got over the fence, he took off the sock that had the dog poop on it. Then he threw it in the woman's neighbors' garbage can. Chris snuck around and got in his car so that he could leave.

He just wanted to go home, but he told Dave that he would stop out at the park and Tori was going to be there, so he left to go meet up with them. Chris got to the park and everyone else was hanging out and having a picnic. When Chris came walking up, he was a mess; he was standing there with one sock on and one sock off. Dave said, "What happened to you?"

"The woman was married, and her husband came home."

"Well that clears up a little. Where are your shoes and why are you wearing one sock?"

"When I got there, she told me that I had to take my shoes off."

"Ok but where's your sock?"

"Well, her husband came home, so I jumped out the bedroom window and when I climbed out of the bush, I stepped in some dog poop."

Lisa asked, "What were you doing in her bedroom, or shouldn't I ask?"

"Her husband came home, so I couldn't go out the front door. So, I had to go out the bedroom window so that he wouldn't see me."

Dave joking asked, "So where is your poopy sock?"

"Really, I threw it in the neighbor's garbage can."

Heather sarcastically said, "Well you probably should've

thrown way that sock too, because it has a hole in it. Oh, by the way, did you at least get paid?'

"Oh yeah, she reached down between her sweaty boobs and took it out of her bra."

Tori said, "Well that is a good place to keep it."

Chris just looked at her and shook his head. Amy giggled and said, "It sounds like you had a shitty appointment."

Chris immediately asked Gary, "Ok what do you have to say?"

"I'm good because they already said everything."

A few days passed and the women started getting appointments. A lot of them were guys that were just trying to get laid, but they just ignored them. Heather, Lisa and Tori each took an address and left for their appointments. Tori arrived at her appointment then went up and knocked on the door. A woman answered and said, "You must be from that cuddle place?"

Tori replied, "Yes."

"Come on in and have a seat." Tori was confused, but she went in and sat down on the couch anyways. The woman said, "My son doesn't have a social life or any friends and just sits around the house all day. Maybe you could help build up his confidence, get him to get a job and move out of my house."

"How old is he?"

"Thirty-five." Then she yelled for her son, "GET OUT HERE!"

When he got out there, she told him, "now you sit down and talk to this pretty woman because someday I'd like to have grandkids. And for heaven's sake, the house to myself. Well I'm going to the store; I'll be back in a little bit."

"It's just a cuddling business." Tori said, "So I'm not allowed to have sex if that's what you're thinking."

"What if there's a really good tip when you're done?"

Tori thought about it, but didn't want to get back into that lifestyle; plus, she kind of liked Chris, had some real friends and didn't want to mess that up. "No, I can't do that."

"Ok whatever." Then she left to go to the store.

Tori moved over by the man and cuddled up next to him. The man got nervous then grabbed the remote for the television and started changing channels. He was a very shy and nervous person. Tori asked, "What kind of television shows do you like?"

"A lot of them."

"Your mom said that you don't have many friends."

"I have no friends, except for the guys that I play online video games with."

"So, you like video games?"

"Yes."

"Do you have a job?"

"I got fired, they said that I didn't have people skills."

"What did you do?"

"I worked customer service at a department store."

Tori felt really weird talking to this guy and kept looking at the time. She asked, "Do you have a girlfriend?" She knew he probably didn't but was trying to be nice and find something to talk about.

The man got a real weird smile, started staring straight ahead and said, "No." Then as he was saying that he started getting a little excited in his man area.

Tori saw that and grabbed a blanket off the back of the couch, covered it up and said, "Think about what you're doing." Then she instantly thought about what she said and told him, "Stop thinking about what you are doing." She could still see that he was excited, so she grabbed a pillow and put it on his lap. Tori said, "I think that we should just sit here and watch television."

The man looked at Tori, then down at his lap, then said, "OK."

Shortly after, his mom got home and asked, "How's everything going?"

"It's going pretty good." Tori said, "You have a very nice son and he's an absolute gentleman." He nervously looked out the corner of his eye and smiled.

Then when time was up, the guy's mom paid Tori and asked, "He's not moving out anytime soon is he?"

"Oh hell no." Then she left to go home.

Heather arrived at her appointment then went up and knocked on the door. A man answered and Heather said, “Hi, I’m Heather from Cuddles.”

“Oh great.” He said, “Come on in.” Then he stuck his head out the door and looked around. “Come over and have a seat.” Then they walked over and sat down on the couch. They started watching television and the man asked, “So what brings you over here?”

“You messaged me to come over.”

“Oh yeah, that’s right.”

Shortly after Heather arrived at her appointment, Lisa arrived at hers.

The man that Heather was cuddling with looked out the window and said, “Shit.”

“Is there something wrong?” The way he acted she thought maybe he had a girlfriend or wife and she was home.

“No, it’s nothing.”

“You don’t have a wife or girlfriend, do you?”

“No, It’s nothing.”

Lisa went up and knocked on the door. A man answered then she said, “Hi, I’m Lisa from Cuddles.”

“Oh, come on in and have a seat.” Then the man stuck his head out the door and started looking around. The man walked over and sat down next to Lisa on the couch.

Lisa asked, “So?”

The man had a confused look on his face and asked, "So what?"

"You messaged me to come over, so I was wondering if there was a reason." The guy that Lisa was cuddling with was acting a little funny also. He was looking out the window and acting very odd. Lisa asked, "Are you expecting someone?"

"No, there's a strange car out there and I'm just keeping an eye on it."

Lisa thought that maybe there was a stranger in the area and he was just making sure that nothing bad was going to happen. Lisa would try to talk to him and he would just look out the window at the car. He would answer her or say something, but he was more worried about the car and he wouldn't make any sense. Lisa asked, "So what made you decide to message us?"

The man replied, "Yes."

Lisa was confused but kept trying to have a conversation. "How did you hear about us?"

"Yeah it's right over there."

Finally, Lisa decided to have a like fun and asked, "Do you eat poop?"

"Yeah but sometimes it gives me a headache."

CHAPTER 12

The guy that Heather's cuddling with kept doing the same thing. He would look out the window and make no sense also. Heather asked, "How was your day?"

"It's down the hall." The man replied, "the first door on the right."

"What's down the hall?"

"Yeah sometimes you have to pull real hard."

"Why do you keep looking out the window?"

"Sure."

Finally, the guy that Heather's cuddling with got up and grabbed his phone, then started texting someone. Heather asked him, "Is there something wrong?"

He smiled and said, "There's nothing wrong."

The guy that Lisa's with continued to look out the window and ignore her. Then he got a text. He got up and grabbed his phone then said, "Oh, hell no."

Lisa asked, "Is there a problem?"

"Not for me." Then he texted whoever texted him and smiled.

The guy that Heather's with received a text then he yelled, "WHAT, YOU GOT TO BE KIDDING ME!"

Once again Heather asked, "Are you sure there's nothing wrong?

The man yelled, "NO THERE'S NOTHING WRONG!" Heather shrugged her shoulders and decided to just sit there. Then the guy texted the person back that texted him.

The guy that Lisa's with once again received a text and said, "Man this can't be happening."

"Is there something wrong now?"

"Yeah, there's some in the kitchen."

Lisa was really confused, but was a little thirsty, so she got up and went into the kitchen to get something to drink. Then she came back into the living room with a glass of milk and a piece of cake.

The guy that Heather's with just kept texting someone back and forth, so she grabbed the remote then started channel surfing. Then she found something that she wanted to watch, so she stopped there to watch the show. Heather asked, “Do you have some chips or something to snack on?”

“Yeah in the kitchen.”

She got up and went into the kitchen to see what he had to snack on.

The guy that Lisa’s with was also caught up into texting someone so she kicked back and found something to watch on television.

All of a sudden, the guy that Heather’s with was getting really frustrated and called the person that he was texting. He said, “Oh this is so good, it’s the best I ever had.”

Then Heather got an idea about what was going on. The guy was apparently telling someone that he was having sex. She just shook her head then continued eating chips and drinking a pop while she watched television.

The guy that Lisa’s with answered the phone and was freaking out. He said, “The best ever, you couldn’t handle what I got going on over here.” Lisa was a little confused but she started to realize what was going on also. She just shook her head and smiled then continued to watch television.

The guy that Heather’s with was still on the phone arguing with someone and kicked over the lamp on the end table. Then he said, “Now my expensive lamps are getting broke.”

Heather looked over at the broken lamp and thought,

"Whatever."

The guy that Lisa's with still was arguing with someone too. All of a sudden, he said, "Oh yeah?" Then he went into the bedroom and started jumping on the bed until it broke. Then he said, "Oh look I just broke my bed."

The man Heather's with put his hand over his phone and said, "Shit, it's getting real over there. It's like two kangaroos over here because we're hopping all over each other."

Heather with a confused look said, "Kangaroos? Don't you mean rabbits?"

"Why would I mean rabbits?"

"Because that's the saying. They're fucking like rabbits."

"I don't really think that's how it goes."

Heather thought to herself whatever and continued doing what she was doing.

Then the man that Lisa's with, held his phone down by his side and said, "They're going at it like two kangaroos."

Lisa with a confused look said, "Kangaroos? Don't you mean rabbits?"

"Kangaroos, rabbits they're all in the same family."

Lisa thought to herself about what an idiot this guy is and continued watching television.

Heather got the guy's attention that she's with and pointed at the clock. Then he said, "Oh you're done, you can't take no more?"

She sarcastically said, "Yeah, I can't take no more now give me my money so I can leave."

The guy that Lisa's with said, "Son of a bitch. Oh, you're done, you can't handle no more of this. Ok I guess if you can't take it no more then we're done."

Lisa said, "Exactly, now give me my money because it's time for me to go."

The guy that Heather's with said, "What? No, you can't spend the night."

Heather and Lisa both motioned for them to pay them so they could leave. Both guys took out their wallets so they could pay them. While they were getting the money, they still continued arguing on the phone and talking nonsense.

The man that Heather's with said, "I can't keep talking to you because I'm about to drop my phone." Then he hung up.

"DON'T YOU HANG UP THAT PHONE!" The man Lisa's with yelled. "He did it, he hung up on me."

Finally, they both hung up so that Heather and Lisa could leave. The guy that Heather's with said, "Thanks" and gave her an awkward hug. Then he walked her to the door so that she could leave.

The guy Lisa's with also said, "Thanks" then went to hug her, but pulled away and stuck out his hand. They shook hands, then he walked her to the door.

As Heather and Lisa were walking out the door, they looked over and saw each other walking out of the houses. They stopped, looked at each other and shrugged their shoulders, while the two guys gave each other angry looks.

Then the guy that Heather was with said, "Oh, I forgot to tip you." He reached into his wallet and grabbed out some more money.

The guy Lisa was with said, "I was just about to tip you before he said that."

The guys kept going back and forth until they had no more money in their wallets. The guy Heather was with tried giving her a coupon for a local burger restaurant. Heather and Lisa walked over to each other and simultaneously said, "That was weird."

Heather said, "I hope it gets better than this."

Lisa replied, "I know, I wonder if this is what the guys went through?"

"We've heard about most of them."

"I guess we did."

"Have a good night."

"Yeah you too."

The two of them walked to their cars and left to go home.

When Heather got home, Dave was sitting on the couch holding Anna. Heather went straight to the couch, grabbed the baby and gave Dave a kiss. Dave asked, "Well?"

"Oh my God."

"That bad?"

"Yes and no." Dave just looked at her with a confused look. She sat down on the couch next to Dave and they snuggled up to each other, then she told him what had happened. "The guy was an idiot and was arguing with the guy that Lisa was with."

Dave with a confused look asked, "What?"

"Lisa was next door at her appointment and then the two of them kept arguing on the phone."

"So, you were next door to each other and didn't even know?"

"Nope, not until we left. We just each took an address and went to our appointments, we didn't even pay attention to it."

"What were they arguing about?"

"They were trying to make each other think that they were having sex."

"You didn't have sex, did you?"

"Oh hell no."

"What did you do while they were arguing on the phone?"

"Watched television, drank a pop and ate some chips."

"Really? Did they pay you?"

"Yep, we both got every dime that they had in their wallets."

"What?"

"Well they paid us, then when we left, they paid us more.

They said that they forgot to tip us, then kept giving us money until they didn't have any more. Oh, then the guy that I was with, tried giving me a buy-one-get-one-free burger coupon."

"I like burgers."

"Well maybe I'll buy you a big juicy burger with all this money that I made tonight." Then the two of them kissed and Heather said, "I love you."

"I love you too."

When Lisa got home, Gary asked, "So how'd it go?"

"Well, let's have a seat." Then they sat down and she explained everything that happened. "The man was really weird."

"I had a few of those."

"What, weird guys?"

"No, you know what I mean. Well, I did have that one guy."

"Ok anyways, he was arguing with someone on the phone about having sex."

"Sex?"

"Yeah I guess they were trying to make the other one jealous or something. The man actually went and broke his bed by jumping on it, to make him think we broke it during rough sex."

"So, you basically got paid to just sit there?"

"Yeah pretty much, well I watched television, ate a piece of cake and drank a glass of milk."

"So, you just walked in the kitchen and made yourself at

home?"

"Yeah I don't even think the guy knew that I went into the kitchen. He pretty much ignored me the whole time. I sure hope it gets better than this."

"I'd like to tell you that it will but from past experiences, you shouldn't count on it."

"That's what I'm afraid of. At least I can come home to you."

The next day at work Dave, Chris and Gary were hanging around at work talking. They were talking about Heather and Lisa's appointments. Chris said, "Really, they just sat there, watched television, ate food and drank?"

Dave and Gary both said, "That's what they said."

Chris said, "I got slobbered on and cuddled with an old lady that talked about screwing her husband to death."

Gary replied, "Don't forget about cuddling with a guy and getting beat up."

Dave said, "At least you and the women have something in common, you both cuddled with dudes." Then Dave and Gary laughed then hi fived each other.

"Very funny, like I said, I don't know if it was a guy and I wasn't going to fight a girl. All I know is, there is no way that we can win this bet."

Dave said, "I agree, because men are always horny."

Chris replied in an angry voice, "See I told you."

Gary said, "So what if we lose, it's something we can do with the women we love."

Chris replied, "You are so whipped."

"Said the single guy," Gary mentioned.

Gary and Dave laughed, then Dave said, "He's got a point."

Chris said, "Ok I'm done with you guys." Then he left to go help a customer.

"Go check the website," Dave told Gary, "I'll be over here helping those people."

CHAPTER 13

After he went to check the website, Gary went to talk to Dave and Chris after they got done helping customers. He said, "Well we got some messages."

Dave said, "See, we can still win this."

Gary replied, "We have appointments, but they have some too."

Chris sarcastically said, "It's no big deal, at least it's something that whipped guys can do with their women."

Dave said, "I'm not whipped, and I don't sound like that. So, I know you're not talking to me."

Gary said, "Not to take anyone's side but you kind of do."

Dave replied, "Says the whipped guy."

Gary said, "I'm not whipped, I just think she makes good

decisions."

Chris said, "Yeah, whipped."

Gary said, "You guys saw her brother."

Chris and Dave both agreed then Dave said, "He's got a point."

Chris said, "Do you think that the women know about their appointments?"

Gary responded, "I texted Lisa and told her check the site."

Chris just made a whipping sound and hand motion. Then they went to help a few customers and to figure out what was going on about the appointments.

When Dave, Chris and Gary got off work, they had two appointments. Chris and Gary were going to go; because Heather had to show a house, then she had an appointment go to. This way, Dave would stay with Anna when Heather went to her appointments. He offered to go to an appointment and Chris could watch Anna, but he respectfully declined.

"Oh hell no."

Dave figured he would say that and that's why he offered to go. Dave remembered the time he watched her before, he had to buy a bottle of spray and a box of wipes. When Dave got home, Heather was leaving to show a house then to her cuddling appointment. He came in, she gave him the baby and a kiss then left. Gary ran home to get ready, then he and Lisa both had to leave. Chris went home, got ready and then he texted Tori and told her, "Good luck on your appointment."

Tori decided to talk shit to him. "Good luck? I'm beautiful, I don't need luck lol."

Chris said to himself, "Yeah, you are beautiful." Then he left to go his appointment.

When Gary got to his appointment, Tori pulled up at the same time. Gary asked, "What are you doing here?"

"I have an appointment here. What are you doing here?"

"I have an appointment here." He grabbed the paper with the address out of his pocket and checked it to make sure it was the right address. Then Tori checked hers and they were both the same. Gary said, "I think I know what's going on, these people are probably swingers and they want to swing with us."

Tori replied, "Think so?"

"Well I guess we'll find out. Why else would they have both of us come?"

"Threesome?"

"WHAT?"

"You know; me, another girl, and you, or you, another guy, and."

Gary interrupted her and replied, "Ok that's enough."

Tori said, "Just saying." They started walking towards the door. Tori decided that she would mess with Gary and ask, "It's been a long time since I've swung or had a threesome, are you ready for this?"

"What? That is against the rules and I'm married."

"It's against the rules, you just couldn't say that you were married?"

"You know what I mean."

"I'm just messing with you, I don't do that stuff no more." Then they walked up and knocked on the door.

After they knocked on the door, a man and woman answered the door. Tori said, "Hi I'm Tori and this is Gary and we're here for the"

Gary knew what she was about to say so he interrupted her and nervously said, "We're here to cuddle from Cuddles, I mean we're from Cuddles to cuddle."

The man and woman replied, "Come on in and have a seat," He introduced himself and his wife to them. He said, "Hi I'm Bill and this is Nancy."

Gary was nervous because since the man and woman were both there, he thought that they wanted to swing. Plus, it didn't help after what Tori said earlier. Gary nervously said, "This is against the rules and I'm married."

The couple looked puzzled. "Excuse my little friend here before he wets himself." Tori said, "We're here to cuddle, so if you expect more than that then we are going to have to decline the invitation."

Bill said, "You think we want to have sex?"

Gary shook his head and Tori just pointed at him. Then he said, "No, we're new here and don't have any friends."

Then Nancy said, "We saw your business and thought that we would give it a try to see about meeting new people."

Bill said, "We were high school sweethearts, I love her and could never picture her with anyone else."

Nancy smiled, kissed Bill on his cheek and said, "Sit down and we'll be right back." Then she and Bill walked into the kitchen.

Bill came into the living room and asked, "Would you guys like something to drink?"

"Yeah, sure."

"Would you like milk, tea or water?"

Tori said, "I'll have some tea."

Gary said, "A glass of water please." Then Bill went back into the kitchen. After a few minutes they came out with a tray full of snacks and the drinks.

Bill and Nancy sat down on the couch then cuddled up next to Gary and Tori. Bill grabbed the remote and started flipping through the channels. He asked, "Is there anything that you guys would like to watch?"

Gary and Tori said, "It doesn't matter."

Nancy said, "We can just sit here and talk so we can get to

know each other."

They all agreed. Gary asked, "So you were high school sweethearts?"

Nancy replied, "Yeah he was my first and only."

Tori asked, "How did you two meet?"

Bill said, "We met on the cheerleading squad."

Gary asked, "You two were cheerleaders?"

Bill replied, "In high school and college."

Tori said, "I used to be a cheerleader."

Nancy replied, "Oh really, and did you marry or date other cheerleaders?"

Tori said, "No, my school didn't have men cheerleaders." Even though she never would've hooked up with any man that was a cheerleader. She said, "Plus I was only a cheerleader in seventh and eighth grades."

Then the woman got excited and whispered into her husband's ear. Then he got excited and said, "That would be great."

Gary and Tori had no idea what was going on, they just looked at each other with puzzled looks.

Bill and Nancy said, "We'll be right back." Then they got up and left the room.

Gary whispered to Tori, "What's going on?"

Tori just shrugged her shoulders and jokingly replied, "Maybe they are going to change into something comfortable, you know; for the orgy."

Gary replied, "I really can't talk to you." Then the couple came back into the living room with their cheerleader uniforms on.

Gary and Tori both sat there with their eyes wide open. Gary said to Tori, "I don't even know what to say."

Tori replied, "Shit, that's what you say."

Bill grabbed the remote and turned off the television. While Nancy went and got a radio then put in a cassette tape. Then they did a cheer. When they were done Bill asked, "Do you guys have any request?" Then he said to Tori, "You have to have one because you were a cheerleader."

Nancy said, "Yes, you have to have a favorite."

Tori said, "I was only a cheerleader in seventh and eighth grade."

Nancy whispered in her husband's ear and he got a big smile on his face. She said, "Then you'll know this one, this was one we did for a pee wee football team."

Gary and Tori just looked at each other while the couple did another cheer. Gary whispered to Tori, "Quit encouraging them." When they were done, they were exhausted, and sat back down on the couch.

Bill asked, "How did you two get into the cuddling business?"

Gary replied, "Me and a couple of my friends decided to do

it to make some extra money."

Tori said, "Well, I used to be a prostitute and Gary's brother in law was going to beat up my pimp."

Bill and Nancy looked at Tori with a confused look. Gary looked at her with an angry look and said, "OK, now tell them the truth." After Tori realized what she said, she quickly changed her story. "I'm just messing with you. I was talking to Gary's friend at the bar, then Gary's wife and her friend needed another woman for their bet."

Nancy asked, "What bet?"

She said, "A bet on who can make more money in a month, the men or the women." Then the couple looked at each other and smiled.

Bill said, "I think we got just what you two need."

Tori replied, "What a gun so we can blow our heads off?"

Bill and Nancy said, "No, a very competitive cheer." Then they stood up and did a cheer. When they were done, Bill said "Bros before hoes." Then he sat down on the couch and cuddled with Gary.

Nancy said, "We got this." Then sat down and cuddled with Tori. Tori and Gary just looked at each other. "Plus, I make more money and can pay you more."

Bill said, "We can't let the women win, just because they got the cooters and threaten to put it away in the box."

Gary looked at him with a weird look and Bill pointed down

at his private area. Gary said, “Oh.”

Nancy said to Bill, “It’s going in the box tonight, after that comment.”

Bill said, “See, I told you.” When time was up, the couple each paid Gary and Tori, then they left.

As they were walking to their cars, Gary said, “And I thought I was whipped.” Then they got into their cars and left.

Lisa showed up at her appointment, then went and knocked on the door. A man answered the door and Lisa said, “Hi I’m Lisa from Cuddles.”

He replied, “Come on in and have a seat.” The man wasn’t a very clean person because he was unnecessarily dirty, he smelled, and the house was a mess.

Lisa went off on him. “You get in there and take a shower and put clean clothes on. No wonder you messaged me, because no woman will ever want anything to do with a dirty man. Unless you just got off work. Did you just get off work?”

He nervously replied, “No, I’m laid off.”

“Really, you’re laid off and your house looks like this? There’s no room to sit on this couch and don’t even think about wanting to go into your bedroom because I can’t even imagine what that looks like. By the way, am I going to get bed bugs if I sit on this couch?”

The man was confused and said, “No, well I don’t think so.”

"You don't know if you have bed bugs?"

"Then, no I don't."

"After you get out of the shower you better get in here and get this living room cleaned or I'm leaving."

By this time the man had second thoughts about it but said, "Ok."

Lisa went to sit in her car until he was done showering and cleaning. "I'll be out in my car, motion for me out the door when you're done."

When the man got done doing everything, he waved out the door for Lisa to come back in.

She went back into the house and the man cleaned it up. "Now this is better." Then the two of them sat down on the couch and cuddled. "Why are you laid off?"

"The company that I worked for went out of business."

"I take it that you don't have a girlfriend."

"She left me because I wasn't looking for a job."

Well you're never going to get her back, or another girlfriend, when you and your house looks like crap and why weren't you looking for a job?"

"Well I lost my job, and my girlfriend left me, so I was depressed then let myself go."

"This is what you're going to do, you're going to look for a job tomorrow."

The man looked at her with a confused look. He couldn't believe that she was talking to him like this and didn't know what to do.

"You're going to clean this whole house tomorrow when you get a few minutes here and there." The man just sat there and listened to Lisa because at this point, he was scared of her. "Then you're going to take the money that you were going to pay me and going to take your ex out to dinner to try to work out your differences."

"You're right and thank you for telling me this stuff. I screwed up and should've done more when my ex was still here. I love her and would do anything to get her back; then when I get a job, I'm going to pay you the money that I owe you."

"You just worry about getting your life in order first."

"Thanks, and as soon as you leave, I'm going to call my ex."

"Good, and I hope it works out for you." Then time was up, he walked her to the door so she could leave. Before she left, she called Gary while he was on his way home from his appointment, to see if he wanted to meet up for dinner. He did, so she left to go meet him to get something to eat.

Heather finished showing the house and went straight to her appointment. When she got there, she went up and knocked on the door. A man came to the door then she said, "I'm Heather from Cuddles."

"Come on in and have a seat." They walked over and sat on the couch. The man sat down and put his head on Heathers shoulder.

"You can put your arm around me, or you can keep your head on my shoulder, whatever you prefer."

The guy opened his eyes real wide with an excited look on his face. Then he sat up with confidence and confidently put his arm around her.

Heather asked, "I'm not judging you, but you don't do this very often, do you?"

The man confidently and sarcastically said, "Um Yeah, all the time."

Heather knew that he was just putting on an act but figured that she would go along with it, since he's paying her to be there. "Do you have a girlfriend?"

"Right now, I'm taking a break and going to wait for the right one. Are you married?"

"No, but I have a boyfriend."

"But you're not married?"

"No, I'm not married."

The man turned his head away from Heather and whispered to himself, "Yes."

Heather said, "Did you say something?"

"No, I just sneezed."

The man's phone rang then he picked it up and looked at it. He said, "I'll be right back." He got up and went to the other side of the room and answered it. He was whispering to someone on the phone so that Heather couldn't hear him. Apparently, the person that he was talking to couldn't hear him either because he kept repeating himself a little louder each time. "She's here right, I said, that she's here." Heather could hear him but acted like she couldn't. She heard the man say, "She's here right now that's why I'm being quiet." He looked at Heather and motioned that he would be over there in a minute. She heard him say, "I didn't think she would come either and guess what? She's not married." Heather could hear everything and had a good guess what the other person was saying. "I'm working on that and don't forget that you're my best man." Then he paused and said, "Duh, you have to know if it's going to be a boy or girl before we can name it." The man looked at Heather, pointed at the phone, shook his head, smiled and shrugged his shoulders. Finally, he got off the phone and went back to sit on the couch.

After he sat down Heather asked, "Is there a problem?"

"No, everything is fine."

"Earlier you said that you haven't met the right woman yet, so how has a man like you not met the right woman?"

He just sat there because he didn't know what to say. Finally, he said, "Well I was engaged and the day before the wedding, she drove her car off a cliff."

"Did she drive her car off a cliff because she didn't want to get married?"

The man realized what he had said, then he instantly changed his story. He said, "No, her brakes went out on the way to the wedding because she was driving really fast to hurry up and get there."

"I'm sorry to hear that, it must have been hard for you."

"Yeah but I dated many other women, so I've gotten over it."

Then Heather noticed the time. "Looks like time is up, I wish I could stay and talk more, but I have stuff to do."

"That's too bad because I had a nice time, guess I should walk you to the door."

"What about my money?"

"Oh yeah, your money." The man took out his wallet and opened it to take the money out. He didn't have any money in there. Heather looked at him with an, oh shit I'm not getting paid look. The man said, "I'll have to get it from my secret hiding spot. You'll have to close your eyes." Heather thought whatever and closed them. Then the man reached down under the couch cushion that Heather was sitting on. He was struggling to get out whatever he was looking for, so he told her, "You'll have to stand up, but keep your eyes closed." Then he held on to her arm when she stood up. "I don't want you to fall while you're standing up because your eyes were closed." Then he reached under the cushion again and grabbed some money. "Ok you can sit back down but you'll have to keep your eyes closed." When she sat down, he told her, "Ok you can open your eyes." Then he handed her the money, smiled and said, "Don't even think about looking for my hiding spot because you'll never find it."

Heather sarcastically said, "Yeah you're probably right so I promise you that I'll never try to find it." Then she left to go home because she had enough stupidity for the day. She just wanted to get home so she could spend time with Dave and Anna.

When Lisa got to the restaurant, Gary was already waiting for her. She parked her car, then she got out and Gary walked into the restaurant with her. As they were walking into the restaurant Gary asked, "How did your appointment go?"

Lisa took a deep breath and just shook her head.

"That bad huh?"

"Well, actually it wasn't that bad." They went into the restaurant then the hostess went and took them to their table. Once they sat down, Gary told Lisa, "Tell me what happened."

"The man and his house were a mess. So, I told him that he would have to clean himself and his house up before I was going to cuddle with him."

"Did you really tell him that?"

"Yes, he stunk, and I wasn't going to sit down by him smelling like that. There wasn't room for two people to sit on the couch. He had clothes, food containers, and dishes all over the couch and coffee table."

"I can't believe that you told him that and he actually did it."

"What does that mean, don't you think I'm worth cleaning up for?"

Gary nervously replied, "Well yeah, you're totally worth it."

Then she smiled and said, "I'm just messing with you. Did you almost wet yourself?"

"No." Then the waitress came over and took their order.

Lisa told Gary to tell her about his appointment. "Well, yours was better."

"No way."

"When I got there, Tori pulled up at the same time. We checked the addresses and they were the same ones."

"Why did you have the same addresses?"

"We figured that it was going to be a couple wanting to swing or have a threesome or something, but it ended up being a couple that was new to the area and had no friends."

"Well I guess that makes sense."

"After we were done, I understood why they had no friends. They were high school sweethearts and they met on the cheerleading squad. Tori mentioned that she used to be a cheerleader, then things got weird."

"That's when things got weird? Meeting on the cheerleading squad wasn't weird enough?"

"Yes, but this was a whole different level of weird." Lisa looked at him with a confused look on her face. "Anyways, after Tori said that she was a cheerleader, they went and put their cheerleading uniforms on."

"Tell me that they didn't do any cheers."

"I wish I could tell you that they didn't, but unfortunately, they did."

"Oh you, poor baby."

"Tori told them about the bet that we have and then they got up and did another cheer for the bet."

"What kind of cheers did they do?"

"I didn't really pay attention because I was trying to think of a non-painful way, I could kill myself. When they were done, the husband sat next to me and his wife sat next to Tori."

"Why did they do that?"

"Bros before hoes and apparently he wanted to help us out and she wanted to help you guys out."

"At first when you said that you and Tori had an appointment together, I thought it would've been cool if it was me and you, but after you said what you did, I think I dodged a bullet."

"Yeah you did." Then they ate their dinner and went on with

their night.

When Heather got home from her appointment, she grabbed Anna out of Dave's hands and gave him a kiss. Dave asked, "So how was your appointment?"

Heather went and grabbed something to drink out of the fridge, then sat down next to Dave on the couch and told Dave about her appointment. "The man was an idiot and thought he was a ladies' man." Dave looked at Heather with a confused look. "I think he thought that we were going to hook up. He actually talked to someone on the phone about marrying me or something like that."

"Did you tell him that you had a boyfriend?"

"Yes, because he asked if I was married, and I said no but I had a boyfriend then the idiot just said, but you're not married."

"Who was he talking to on his phone?"

"I don't know, apparently another idiot. He was trying to whisper so I couldn't hear him, but he was too quiet, and his friend couldn't hear anything. Then he whispered loud enough so his friend could hear him, but I could kind of heard him too."

"Did you get paid?"

"Yes, he got the money from his secret hiding spot."

"How did you know that it was his secret hiding spot?"

"Because he told me; by the way his hiding spot is under the far left couch cushion." Dave just looked at her. "He made me close my eyes so I wouldn't see his secret hiding spot. Then he started digging under the couch cushion that I was sitting on. Oh, get this, he couldn't get the money out, so he had me stand up so he could get it."

"And he never realized what he was doing?"

"No, I'm so glad that I have you in my life."

Tori was sitting around and didn't have anything going on, so she texted Chris to see if he wanted to go out for a drink or something. Chris was watching television and didn't have anything to eat so he told her that he would meet up with her. "Where do you want to go?"

"I don't know, what do you think?"

"Mexican sounds good. How about the Mexican restaurant across town?"

"That's fine, give me a few minutes to get ready and I'll meet you there."

"Ok, I'm going to get ready and I'll see you in a little bit." Chris was done and headed towards the door, then he stopped and said, "Oh shit." He took out his wallet and pulled out his gift card and said, "Oh good." Then he left to go meet Tori. Chris got there before Tori did, so he texted her and told her to text him when she got there. She texted him back and said that she would be there in a few minutes. About ten minutes later, Tori got to the restaurant and texted Chris to tell him that she was there. Then he got out of his car and waited for her so they could walk in together. "A few minutes, that was like ten minutes."

"Ten minutes is a few minutes for a woman, plus you can't rush perfection."

Chris just looked at her and shook his head. Then she started walking toward the door. Chris stood there for a second and whispered, "Damn she is perfect." Then he followed her to the door so they could go in and get seated.

When they got seated, the waitress took their drink orders and said that she would be right back. When she went to get their drinks, Chris asked, "How did your appointment go?

"Oh geez."

"That good huh?"

"I've met some weird or messed up people in my life, but this couple had to be the weirdest."

"Couple?"

"Yeah a husband and his wife."

"You cuddled with both of them?"

"Well kind of." As they were talking, the waitress brought their drinks and to take their orders. They were busy talking, so they really weren't ready to order yet. Tori rushed through the menu to hurry up and order while the waitress waited. She asked Chris, "Didn't you say the tacos here were to die for?"

Chris looked at the waitress with an embarrassed look shaking his head, "No I said that the burritos were really good, I never said anything about to die for."

"Whatever, I'll take the tacos."

The waitress looked at Chris, "I'll have the burritos." The waitress took their menus and went to put their order in. "I said the burritos were really good, your pimp said that he had tacos."

"Really?"

"I was just clearing things up."

"Do you want to hear about my appointment?"

"Ok tell me about your appointment."

"When I got there, Gary pulled up about the same time and we had no idea what to expect."

"You and Gary had the same appointments?"

"Yes, it was a couple new to the area and they didn't have any friends so they messaged us to come over."

"That's not weird because a lot of people move, and it takes time to meet people."

"They were high school sweethearts and they met on the cheerleading squad."

"What's weird about that? Well, I guess the cheerleading thing can be a little weird."

"They cheered for us."

Chris looked at her with a confused look and asked, "Cheered?"

"They went and put on their old cheerleading uniforms and

did cheers."

"Ok that's weird at a whole different level."

Then she finished telling him about the appointment while they ate. "Then I mentioned the bet, so the woman's husband cuddled with Gary and she cuddled with me."

"This may be a stupid question, but why?"

"I guess because they felt that they were doing us both a favor by the man supporting the men and the woman supporting the women."

"Actually, that might be weird to you but that actually would have been considered a good appointment for me."

"I've heard about some of the appointments that you went on, did you have other bad ones?"

"Other bad ones? "I've had a lot of bad ones. I cuddled with a perverted old woman, a bigger woman that apparently loves barbeque sauce, I got stung by bees and got bullied by kids. Oh, then cuddled with a guy or ugly woman I couldn't really tell."

"How did you not know if someone was a man or a woman?"

"Do you remember when we met at the bar and Heather asked you about cuddling?"

"Yeah."

"Do you remember the woman or whatever that was standing there when you got back from the restroom?"

"That was her?"

"Yes."

"Well, I actually think she's a woman."

"How do you know?"

"Well later that night I went to the restroom again and she followed me in there. Then she sat in the stall next to me and kept telling me to stay away from you."

When they finished eating, they continued to talk while they finished their drinks. "Why did you get into prostitution I don't mean to be nosy or anything, and if you don't want to talk about it you don't have to."

"I had a rough childhood and thought it was a way out and to make money."

"You are a very beautiful woman and I was wondering why you felt that you had to do it."

"Thanks, and I regretted it, but was scared to try to get out of it. Then after what Lisa's brother said to him, I decided to tell him that I wasn't working for him anymore. If there was going to be a problem, I was going to find Lisa's brother, and make something up so that he would kick his ass. He got scared and told me to leave. Then I went to the club hoping to see you guys there so that I could apologize to you."

Then the waitress brought the bill and Tori went to give Chris some money for what she ordered. Chris said, "Don't worry, I got it."

"That's right, you have a gift card for this place."

As she was saying that, Chris was going through his wallet and had his fingers on the gift card. Then he took them off the card and said, “What do you think I’m cheap?” Then he reached back into his wallet and turned his body so Tori couldn’t see what he was doing. He took out the gift card with some money and handed it to the waitress. He whispered to the waitress, “I don’t know how much is on the card, but there’s some money to cover the difference.” He didn’t want to be cheap and wanted to show off, so he told the waitress, “Keep the change.”

They walked outside and Tori gave him a hug then told him, “Thanks for dinner.” Then they walked to their cars and went home.

CHAPTER 14

The next day Dave, Chris and Gary all had to work. Gary told them about his appointment with the cheerleaders. He said, “I had the weirdest appointment yesterday.”

“Yeah I heard, Tori told me last night.”

“Wait, Tori told you?” Dave asked, “Did she come over your apartment?”

“No, we were just sitting around so we thought that we would go get something to eat and have some drinks.”

Gary said, “So you went out on a date?”

“No, we didn’t go out on a date, it was just two people having dinner and drinks.”

Dave said, “Did you pay?”

“Yes.”

"Then it was a date," Dave said.

Gary asked Chris, "So are you two a couple now?"

"No, we're not a couple and it wasn't a date."

Gary said, "I know that I don't have a lot of experience with this stuff, but to me, it sounds like a date."

Dave looked at Chris and shrugged his shoulders then pointed at Gary. Chris said to Gary, "You know, ever since you got married you've became a real smartass."

Gary asked Dave, "Was I wrong?"

Dave replied, "No, he's just in denial that he has a girlfriend." Then Dave and Gary both started singing, "Chris and Tori sitting in a tree."

Before they could finish Chris said, "I can't deal with you two and how old are you guys anyways?" Then he walked away to go help some customers.

After Chris left, Dave and Gary kept talking. Gary said, "I think he's mad."

"He's always mad, he'll get over it. So how did Lisa's appointment go?"

Gary told Dave about Lisa's appointment. "She made the man take a shower and clean his house before she'd cuddle with him."

"What?" Dave smiled and asked, "I hope that you never come home dirty."

"Oh, she let me know what was up when we first started dating."

"You really are whipped."

"Well she is the first woman that I've went out with."

"And you did the right thing and married her."

"What would you have done if Heather would've told you what Lisa told me?"

"Well, I would've had sex with her and if she didn't like me the way I was, then I probably would've moved on." Gary looked at Dave with a surprised look on his face. "I'm just busting your balls and I would've done the same thing as you. I love both of you guys and I couldn't ask for better friends."

"Me and Lisa feel the same way about you and Heather. Oh yeah, how did Heather's appointment go?"

"Well I guess the guy was an idiot. He thought that he was some stud and was going to hook up with Heather."

Later that night, the women had more appointments. Heather arrived at her appointment, then she went up and knocked on the door. After a few minutes a man came and answered the door and she said, "Hi, I'm Heather from Cuddles." He just sat there and smiled. Heather asked, "Can I come in?"

"Oh yeah, come in."

She went in the house and the man just stood there staring at her. She finally asked, "Do you want to go and sit down?"

"Yeah sure." Then he walked over and sat in a chair.

Heather looked at him with a confused look and sat down on the couch. "Do you want to come over here?"

"Do I?"

Heather thought to herself, not again. "Yes, I think you do, unless you want to pay me to sit across the room from you." The man sat there thinking about it.

"Are you thinking about it?"

"Yeah."

Heather thought to herself that this guy really can't be this stupid, but after the first guy, she wouldn't doubt it. Heather asked, "Is there a problem?"

"Well kind of."

She sat there for a second waiting for the man to tell her, but he just sat there. "Would you like to tell me about it?"

"No. Ok, sometimes I wet myself when I get nervous." Heather regretted asking him but told him that it would be fine for him to come over and sit on the couch. The man thought about it for a second then he got up and went to sit next to Heather.

The man sat down on the other side of the couch. Heather looked at him and patted the couch next to her for him to move over by her. Then she said, "Don't worry, I don't bite." Then the man got a weird look on his face. "Did you just pee?"

"Yeah."

"Really, just like that?"

"Well what you said was kind of sexy."

"What, about not to worry because I don't bite?" The man instantly had the same face that he had when he wet his pants the first time. "Did you just do it again?" The man just sat there looking around and ignored what Heather asked him. "Are you going to go change your pants?" The man just looked at her. Then she said, "Yes you are going to change."

"Oh, ok." Then he got up to go and change his pants.

Heather said to herself, "Now I know how Chris felt."

The man came back wearing clothes that didn't match. Heather didn't say anything because he had clothes that didn't smell like pee. The man walked in the kitchen and turned on the water.

Heather asked, "What are you doing?"

"Getting a drink."

"Do you think that's a good idea?"

"But I'm thirsty." He walked out into the living room with a glass of water.

"Ok, how about you put the glass on the table, then when I leave, drink the water."

"But I'm thirsty now."

"If you drink that, then you might wet yourself again. Right now, the well's empty." He looked back and forth at Heather and the glass of water then he put it on the table. Heather said, "You did the right thing."

The man looked at the clock and said, "Oh it looks like time's up." Heather sat there wondering what was going on, because they never cuddled and it hadn't even been an hour. The man said, "I'll have to get your money but it's in a secret hiding spot."

Heather thought to herself, not again.

The man said, "You'll have to close your eyes." Heather sat there and closed her eyes. The man started making faces and doing weird motions in front of her to see if she was looking. After he realized that she wasn't, he started reaching under the cushion that she was sitting on. He couldn't get the money out because Heather was sitting on the cushion. "Could you stand up, but you'll have to keep your eyes closed." After she stood up, he got the money from under the cushion and said, "You can sit back down, but keep your eyes closed." After she sat down, he said, "You can open your eyes now."

Heather opened them and then the guy handed her the money. The money was all crumpled up and Heather didn't even know if there was enough there, but at this point she just wanted to leave. She also thought that they didn't even cuddle, so she didn't care. She said, "Thanks."

"No problem, you're welcome."

"Don't worry about getting up because I can let myself out."

Then she left to go home.

When Tori arrived at her appointment, it was a mansion. She thought why the hell was this guy messaging her to come cuddle. Tori was debating on going up to the door because she thought that maybe the guy wanted to have sex. She knew that she couldn't do that anymore because she didn't want to get the business shut down. Plus, she liked Chris and didn't want to mess up any future that they might have. She decided that she would go up there, and if he wanted to have sex then she would just leave. She walked up and knocked on the door and a butler answered the door. Tori said, "Hello, I'm Tori from Cuddles."

"We've been expecting you. Come on in and follow me." When they got to the living room there was a man sitting on the couch and the butler announced, "This is Tori from Cuddles."

"Come on over and sit down."

She walked over and sat down next to him. "Why did you message me to come over here to cuddle with you if you own all this?"

"It's not my house, it's actually my parents'."

"I don't care who owns it, you should have women crawling all over you."

"That's the problem, women either are too good for me or not good enough for me and just want my parents' money. I just want to have a nice conversation with an average woman."

Tori didn't know if she should take that as an insult or not. She figured it wasn't, then sat there and talked to the man.

"My parents are out of town, so I thought I'd give your business a try. I don't get out much and could use the company."

"Well, you should get out more."

"I'm tired of going to country clubs, foreign resorts or celebrities' mansions."

"There are other places to go and things to do. You can go see a movie, local beach or a dance club."

"I don't know if I would fit in if I went to any of those places."

"You'd be fine, but you need to get out more. That way you won't have to pay someone to come over and hang out. Apparently, it's not like money's a problem."

"It's not." Tori and the man sat there and talked. The man was a little different because he wanted to talk about money and politics, which was stuff that Tori knew nothing about. Well, she knew how to spend money, but knew nothing about politics. "So, do you invest in the stock market?"

"No."

"What do you do with your money?"

"Spend it."

"On what?"

"Clothes, make up, stuff like that."

"You really should look into investing it so that you can have money to retire with."

"Yeah, I really don't make enough money for that."

"Are you Republican or Democrat?"

"Actually, I don't get into politics."

"Politics is a very important part of our society."

"You really need to get out more, and if you do, don't talk about money or politics."

"What should I talk about."

"Movies, food, what people do for a living, but it's movies, food and jobs that normal people watch or have."

"I don't know anything about that stuff?"

"Look it up online."

The butler came into the living room and said, "Time's up."

The man got his wallet out, paid her and said, "Thanks for coming."

"It's no problem, and there's a club in town that I go to, it's called BJ's. You should go up there once in a while and get out of the house."

"Maybe I will."

"If you do and I'm up there with my friends, stop and say hi."

"I'll do that." Then the butler walked her to the door so she could leave.

Lisa arrived at her appointment, then went up and knocked on the door. A man answered and Lisa said, "Hi, I'm Lisa from

Cuddles."

"Oh great, come on in and sit down." Lisa went in and sat down on the couch then the man sat in a chair across from the couch. Lisa was confused because he didn't sit down next to her. "I messaged you because my dad could use some company."

"This is just a cuddling business and we don't have sex with anyone."

"Oh no, that's not what I mean. My dad isn't doing good, ever since my mom passed away."

"Sorry to hear about your mom, how long has it been since she passed?"

"Oh it's been a long time, but my dad really needs to get over it." Lisa looked at him with a confused look on her face. "I shouldn't say that, but he needs to get out and do things."

"People grieve differently than others. My parents both passed away in a car accident and there's not a day that goes by that I don't think about them."

"Sorry to hear about your parents and I didn't mean it that way. I love my dad and want the best for him, and maybe getting out more often would do him some good. Anyways, he's in his bed and hardly ever gets out of it. Is it alright if you went in there and hung out?"

"That would be fine."

The man walked Lisa to his dad's bedroom and introduced

her to him. "Dad, this is Lisa and she's here to hang out and talk for a little while." The man was sitting up in his bed watching television.

"Can I sit down and hang out for a little bit?"

"Sure."

Lisa got in the bed then watched television with him. He was watching a documentary about World War II. Lisa asked, "Were you in the military?"

"Yes, I was."

"Thank you for your service."

"No problem, it had to be done. I've seen a lot of bad things, but I would do it all over again if I had to, with no regrets." They talked about what it was like to grow up back in those days. "Back then there wasn't much to do so after you graduated from school, you went to the military. It's not like kids now a days that have phones and their video games. My dad and grandpa were in the military so I came from a military family. Was any of your family in the military?"

"No."

"Me and my two best friends all went in the military together and only two of us came back."

"Sorry to hear that."

"Me and Bobby both went into the Marines and our friend Jerry went to the Army. Jerry wanted to come with us in the Marines, but his dad was in the Army, so he decided that's what he was going to do. Then one day after the war, we came home and went to see if Jerry was on leave, then his dad told us the bad news."

"I'm sorry to hear that, but Jerry died a hero."

"Yes, he did and he sure was."

Then he started to talk about how he met his wife. Lisa really hoped that he wouldn't bring her up, but she figured that he would. He told Lisa about how they met when he was on leave from the military. "It was actually that time when I met my wife. Me and Bobby met her in a bar when we were celebrating Jerry's life. She told me that I better not go and get myself killed because she wanted to see me again. She was beautiful so that was my motivation to make sure that I made it back."

"You really loved your wife?"

"Yes, I did. My life has never been the same since she got sick and passed away."

"Your life isn't going to be the same when you lose a loved one, but it can still be a great life. You can't worry about the past because you've got a son that's worried about you."

"Yeah I suppose he is."

"Is your son married, and does he have any children?"

"Yes, I have a beautiful daughter-in-law and a grandson."

"See, don't miss out on what you have now, worrying about the past. I'm sure your wife would not want you to sit around and do nothing. She would want you to go out and enjoy yourself."

"I suppose she would, because she was a very unselfish woman."

"How old is your grandson."

"He's five."

"There you go, you're all going to take a family trip to the park and have a picnic. That's just for starters, because you have the zoo, school functions, and many other things to do before you miss out on anything else." The man just looked at Lisa and smiled. "I'm not taking no for an answer."

The man replied with a smile, "I guess that I have no choice then."

"No, you don't, because I know where you live."

As she was getting ready to leave the man asked, "Can I give you a hug?"

"I wasn't leaving without one. Oh, and you better be a gentleman and give me a peck on my cheek."

"I wasn't giving you a hug without one." Then Lisa walked out of the room and went into the living room to talk to his son.

He asked, "How'd it go?"

"It went great, and he agreed to get out more often." Lisa replied with a smile, "You guys already have a picnic date set up at the park."

He smiled and said, "Oh yeah, that sounds great. As soon as my wife gets home, we can plan something and thanks for everything." The man took out his wallet and paid her, then he walked her to the door. As she was walking to her car he said, "Thanks again."

Lisa stopped and jokingly replied, "If he gives you any more problems, you know where to find me." Then she continued to walk to her car and left.

While the women were at their appointments Dave, Chris, and Gary went to hang out at the park with Amy. Then when the women got done with their appointments, they were going to meet them there. Heather was going to pick up some pizzas when she got finished so Amy wouldn't have to cook anything. While they were waiting for the women, they sat around and talked. Amy asked, "How is the bet going?"

Dave said, "Well, not good."

"I take it you three are losing?"

Chris answered, "We never stood a chance."

Amy said, "Well, men are pushy and always horny."

Chris said to Dave, "See, I told you."

Gary mentioned, "It doesn't matter to me if I win or not, it gives me and Lisa something else that we can do together."

Chris said to Gary, "How does Lisa sit down with your nose up her ass?"

Dave replied, "You'll find out soon."

Chris asked, "What does that mean?"

"Pretty soon your nose will be up Tori's ass." Dave answered.

Chris said, "Get out of here."

Amy asked, "What, do you have a thing for Tori?"

Gary said, "They went out on a date."

Amy asked, "Oh really?"

Chris said, "It wasn't a date, we just met for dinner and drinks."

Amy asked, "Who paid?"

Chris replied, "I did."

Then Amy said, "Well that sounds like a date to me."

Dave shrugged his shoulders and pointed at Amy because he agreed with what she said. "Well, when Tori gets here, we can ask her."

Chris said to Dave, "You're not going to say anything to Tori." Gary got ready to say something and Chris interrupted him. "You're not going to say anything either. You just sit there and do the whole I love my wife thing." Chris said to Amy, "Don't get me started with you."

Dave, Gary and Amy all laughed. Dave said, "I figured you would be a little nicer when you got a girlfriend."

Chris said to Dave, "Don't, just don't."

CHAPTER 15

Shortly after the men got there the women were getting done with their appointments. Lisa was going to pick up something to drink and meet Heather at the pizza place so she could help with the pizzas. Tori went straight to the park when she left, so she got there first. When she arrived, Dave said to her, "So how was your day?"

Tori replied, "Good."

Chris mumbled to Dave, "Don't."

Tori asked Dave and Gary, "Did you guys talk to Heather or Lisa?"

They said, "No but they should be getting here soon."

Chris asked Tori, "How was your appointment?"

"It wasn't bad. It was a rich guy that don't get out much."

"Rich, is he single?" Amy asked.

"Yes he is."

Dave said, "There you go, if you haven't been out on a date in a while then there's your chance."

Tori replied, "Well I was kind of on a date yesterday."

Gary said to Chris, "See, you said it wasn't a date." Chris shook his head rolled his eyes.

Tori asked Chris, "What did you tell them?"

"I just told them that we met up for drinks and had dinner. Then these idiots all started talking about it being a date."

"Well you did pay so I guess it was kind of a date."

Amy said, "She's beautiful, you should be happy that you went out on a date with her."

Tori asked Chris, "What, I'm not pretty enough for you and you were embarrassed to go out with me?"

"No, you are beautiful. See what you guys started." Then Heather and Lisa came walking up with the pizzas. Chris said, "Look who's here, anybody else hungry?"

Amy was holding Anna and she needed her diaper changed as Heather came walking up. Amy said, "Just in time, somebody left you a little surprise." Amy handed Anna over to Heather.

Heather asked Chris, "Do you want to change this?"

Dave said, "Oh hell no, because I don't feel like going to the store to buy more baby wipes tonight."

Chris asked, “You wanted her clean, didn’t you?”

Heather said, “No, I got this.” Then she said to Dave, “Well we do need more diapers.”

Chris said to Dave, “There you go, smartass.”

Tori asked, “Why are you so hateful and mean?” Then everyone laughed.

“So, she’s one of you guys now and it’s gang up on Chris day.” Chris said, “I get it, give me some pizza.”

Heather went to change Anna and everyone else started to eat. When they were done, they all walked out to their cars together. When they were walking to their cars, Lisa saw the old man and his son from her appointment earlier. They were sitting on a blanket and having a picnic with the whole family. The man’s son looked over and saw Lisa and waved to her. Gary asked, “Who is that?”

“It’s the man from my appointment from earlier. I’ll tell you about it on the ride home.”

The next day, Dave and Gary had to work. It was a slow day, so they were just standing around talking. “Let’s go check the web site.” Dave said, “Maybe there will be like fifty appointments, then maybe we can catch the women.”

Gary replied, “Even if we had fifty then the women would have one hundred.”

“That’s true, it was something we got to do with them and

now they know what the business is like."

"It doesn't have to end, just because the bet was a month why not have them keep doing this with us?"

"Yeah I'd like that."

"It gave me and Lisa something else we can do together and stuff to talk about."

"It let Heather and I see what other people are going through so we can use that to help us out in our relationship. Let's go check the web site and we can talk to the women about this at the end of the month." Then Dave and Gary went to check the computer. When they checked there was one message, but there was also one for the women. The guys never check the women's, so Dave asked Gary, "Do you want to text Lisa and see if she knows that there's a message?"

"She's working, so why don't you text Heather and let her figure things out."

"I'll text Heather, and you text Chris to see if he wants to go since he's home."

Chris never saw the message, but he told Gary, "I'll check it out and can go." Chris messaged the woman back and said, "I can come over anytime."

She eventually messaged back and said, "I won't be home until around seven o'clock."

Chris messaged back, "I'll be over around seven fifteen."

Chris had plenty of time before he had to get ready to go, so he watched television and enjoyed the rest of his day off. Then the time came where Chris had to start getting ready so he could leave. After he was ready, he left to go to his appointment.

When he got to the woman's house he walked up and knocked on the door. Then a goth woman answered the door and Chris just looked at her. She said to Chris, "Can I help you?"

"I'm sorry, hi, I'm Chris from Cuddles."

"I figured that's who you were but there are some weird people in this world, so I wanted to make sure."

"Well come on in." Chris walked in behind the woman and they walked over to the couch then sat down. They just sat there and watched television.

Chris felt a little uncomfortable because they weren't talking and just sitting there. He decided to start a conversation. Chris asked with a smile, "I'm not here for a virgin sacrifice, am I?"

The woman replied with serious look, "No, I'm goth not a gypsy, into voodoo or in a cult."

Chris felt weird after her response, so he said, "Well that's good because I'm not a virgin anyways."

Once again with a serious look she said, "Are you serious?"

By this time Chris was feeling really uncomfortable. "Yeah I've been with many women, as a matter of fact I met a friend at a Mexican restaurant across town."

"Did you sleep with her?"

"No, we just met up for dinner and drinks."

"Oh, you just met up with a friend."

"No, I paid, so it was a date."

"Just because you paid doesn't mean it was a date."

"That's exactly what I tried to tell them!" He replied with excitement, "But no, I paid so it had to have been a date!"

"Friends pay for their friends all the time."

Then Chris said with a smile, "Well that's good to know that you're not going to sacrifice a virgin or a chicken or anything because I'm not chicken either."

The woman with a serious face asked, "Are you sure?"

Chris was confused and asked," Sure about what?"

"That you're not a chicken."

Chris paused and looked at her with a confused look and said, "Of course, look at me, I'm clearly a human."

"Do you want to fight my brother?"

With another confused look Chris asked, "No, why would I want to fight your brother?"

"Well, you sound like a chicken to me."

Chris was really confused and had no idea where she was going with all of this. "I'm not a chicken, I have no reason to fight your brother. I don't know your brother he could be a really great guy."

"No, he's an asshole so do you want to fight him now?"

Chris didn't know what to say. "Just because he might be an asshole doesn't mean that I want to fight him, I might not think he's an asshole."

"Well you just called him an asshole."

"No, I never said that."

"You said just because he might be an asshole doesn't mean you want to fight him."

"Then I said that I might not think he's an asshole."

"Oh, I didn't hear that part."

"What made you message us anyways?"

"I don't have many friends and thought I'd try it out to see what it was like. I figured it would be nice to have someone to talk to and hang out with, then if I like it, I'll do it every day."

"That would get really expensive."

"This costs money?"

"What?"

"This costs money?"

"Yeah, it says it right on the web site."

"I probably should have put my glasses on when I read it." Chris just rolled his eyes and shook his head. "I'm just messing with you I know it costs money. I'm kind of spoiled and my parents have money,"

"Do you even have a brother?" She replied, "Yeah I do and

he's an MMA fighter."

"And you wanted me to fight him?"

"Oh no because he'd kill you. I did tell you the truth about me not having many friends and messaging you for someone to hang out with."

"There's a club in town called BJ's, have you ever been there?"

"No, I haven't been to that one."

"You should check it out, it will get you out of the house and maybe you could meet some new people."

"I might check it out one day."

"Well if you do and I'm there, then make sure you say hi."

"I could probably do that. Well I guess your time is up, and I'll be right back with your money." She got up and went to get Chris his money. She came back into the living room, paid him, and said, "Thanks for the conversation."

"No problem." Then she walked Chris to the door so he could leave.

Heather never saw the message and thanked Dave for telling her. "I'll get ahold of Lisa and Tori and see what they want to do."

They both said to Heather, "If you can and want to, then you can go." Lisa was working and didn't want to rush home after work, and Tori wasn't feeling well.

"That's fine." Then she texted Dave back to tell him to come straight home after work because she was going on the appointment. Heather never read the message before she texted everyone, so she decided to check it. It said at the end of the message to bring a bathing suit. Heather was confused, apparently the guy wanted to cuddle in a pool or something. Anyways she messaged back and said that she would be there. She continued doing what she was doing and waited until it was time for her to get ready to leave. When Dave got home, Heather got ready and left for her appointment.

When she got to the address, it was a really nice house. She thought why is this man paying someone to come and cuddle? She walked up and knocked on the door. A beautiful woman answered the door and Heather said, "I must have the wrong address."

She asked, "Are you looking for Mark?"

"Yes."

"He's in the back yard, so you can just walk around through that gate."

Heather walked around to the back yard and there were a bunch of really hot women hanging around back there. Then some really good looking and muscular man stood up out of the hot tub then he introduced himself. "Hi I'm Mark. You must be from the cuddle place?"

"Yes, and I'm Heather."

"There's a changing room right over there, you can go in and get changed, then we'll hang out in the hot tub."

After Heather put her bathing suit on, she walked over and got into the hot tub. Mark moved over by her and cuddled up next to her. When he did, he flexed his pectoral muscles and said, "WHOA those things have a mind of their own." He smiled and did it a few more times. Even though Heather thought that the man was nice looking, she thought that he was really annoying. He asked, "Would you like something to drink?"

"No thanks." Mark insisted that she have a drink, so he called one of the women over to go and get them a couple of drinks. She went over to the bar then made their drinks and took the drinks to them. They sat there cuddling in the hot tub and having a drink. Heather asked Mark, "Why did you message us if you had all these women already here?"

"Because I see these women and have sex with them any time I want to. Yeah, they're all beautiful women, but I thought that it would be nice to just hang out with an average woman." She looked at him with a confused look. "No disrespect, you're a pretty woman, but let me guess, you have a nice-looking boyfriend and a child?"

"Lucky guess."

"No not lucky, look at your body I can tell that body gave birth to a little human." Heather looked down at her body with sad look. "I have a gorgeous boyfriend, a beautiful baby girl and a nice body for having both of those."

He smiled at her and said, "That's cute." Then he started to flex his pectorals again. "I don't know why these things are so jumpy tonight."

Even though Mark was arrogant they sat there, had a few drinks and talked. "Dave may not be rich but he's a great guy and father, and he gave me a beautiful baby girl."

"I used to be a professional body builder and now I own a few gyms, but I wish I had Dave's life."

"You have all this, why would you want an average person's lifestyle?"

"I've always had hot women, but it would be nice to have a woman that I can actually have a conversation with. That's why I messaged you. To be honest, I was hoping that cuddling meant cuddling and not a cover up for sex."

"You're good, but what if it was?"

"I'd have sex, especially if I was paying for it. "Are you getting at something?"

"Oh no."

Mark let out a deep breath and said, "Good." Heather looked at him with a confused look. "See these beautiful women around here, none of them have kids. If I had sex with someone that had kids, then that would be like having sex with my mom."

"Well that has nothing to do with each other, but I get it." Then time was up, so Mark yelled over at one of the girls to get him his wallet. She brought his wallet to him, then he got Heather's money out and paid her. After he paid her, he handed his wallet back to the girl to put it back. As Heather was getting out of the hot tub, Mark smiled and once again flexed his pectoral muscles.

"I have no idea what got into those tonight." Heather rolled her eyes, shook her head and continued to get out of the hot tub so that she could get dressed then leave. When she got dressed, she left to go home so that she could hug Dave and hold Anna.

It was the end of the month, and of course the women won the bet. They all decided that they would go to the club to celebrate. Gary's mom was watching Anna so that Dave and Heather could go out. They got her to babysit so that Amy could go and hang out with them for the night. When they all got there, Dave ordered a round of drinks and did a toast. "Even though you kicked our asses, it was fun, and I love you all." Then they all hugged, kissed or shook hands.

Chris said, "I told you that they would win."

Then everyone sarcastically said to Chris, "We know; because men are pushy and always horny."

Chris replied, "Really, you're all going to gang up on me now?" They hung around the bar, talked, listened to the music and drank.

As they were standing there the rich man came running by

them, then he noticed Heather, stopped and went back to where she was standing. He was all hyper and said, “Thanks for telling me about this place, it’s amazing and the beautiful women.” As he was talking a new song came on then he said, “Oh my God, I love this song.” Then he took off running to the dance floor.

Everyone just looked at Heather with a confused look. “It was someone that I cuddled with, I told him he needed to get out.”

Dave replied, “I definitely think you were right.”

Gary said, “I thought I was bad.”

Lisa said to Gary, “Yeah, but I took care of that.”

Gary was just talking to everyone and someone came up behind him. It was the couple that he cuddled with before. Gary said, “Hey, how have you guys been?”

“We’ve been great.”

“That’s good, this is my wife Lisa.”

“It’s nice to meet you.”

The wife said, “That’s great, you’re not a virgin anymore.”

Lisa looked at Gary with a confused look and Gary embarrassingly said. “I’ll tell you later.”

The husband said, “Thanks to you, we’ve met some real nice people.”

“It’s nice to hear that everything is working out for you two.”

Then the husband said, “We’ve had so much.”

Gary knew exactly what he was going to say and interrupted

him. "Ok, we really don't need to know any details."

The wife said, "Well we are meeting some new friends tonight so we really should go."

"It was nice seeing you guys."

Lisa said, "It was nice to meet you."

They both said, "It was nice meeting you, Lisa, and seeing you guys."

As they started to walk away the wife said, "Maybe we should meet up sometime?"

Lisa said, "That would be."

Gary interrupted her and said, "Well we are really busy, and we'll have to get back with you guy on that."

She said, "Ok, you take care."

Lisa said to Gary, "What's wrong with you?"

"Well they wanted to have sex with us."

"What?"

"They are swingers and wanted to have sex with us."

"Eww, how do you know them?"

"That's the couple that I cuddled with that wanted to see how it felt for them to cuddle with strange people."

"Oh, apparently it felt pretty good."

Dave, Heather and Amy were talking while Gary was talking with the couple. Dave said to Amy, "I, I mean we, want to thank you for everything and we are really glad that you're in our lives."

"I should be thanking you, because you filled that void that I've had in my life since my husband passed."

Heather said, "Yeah but you've been great to Anna and she really loves you."

"Yeah and the times that me and Heather went through our problems, you were there for us, the picnics."

"That's what friends do, and I just love Anna to death. The picnics are because I like to cook and enjoy you guys' company." Then Amy pointed at everyone else and said, "I even love these guys and it was great that you brought me into your lives." Then Dave, Heather and Amy had a group hug.

Chris was talking to Tori and Lucy came walking up behind him and whispered in his ear. "Hey there."

"WHAT THE HELL?" He turned around and pulled his head back then said, "Really, you have to sneak up behind be and scare the shit out of me?"

"I surprised you, I didn't scare you."

"No, you definitely scared me, and as a matter of fact, you're still scaring me."

Tori said to Chris, "I'll be back, I got to go to the restroom."

Lucy said, "I never thought that she would leave."

Chris asked, "What do you want?"

"I missed you."

"Missed me? We cuddled one time."

"It was twice, but I can see in your eyes that you can't quit thinking about it."

"Ok I just threw up a little in my mouth and I'm actually about to throw up all over the floor."

"You are so silly. I'm going to go dance then you'll be all over me." As she was saying that, she was dancing around, and Chris started to gag. Lucy walked away to go dance.

The two idiot men that Heather cuddled with came walking up, saw Heather, and said, "Hey there."

Heather saw them both together and said, "Now this all makes sense." Now she knew who the one guy was talking to when he was on the phone, when they cuddled. She looked at them and introduced Dave to them. "This is my boyfriend, Dave."

The one man said to his friend, "See, I told you that she wasn't married."

Then they started to walk away, and the other man said, "She is so into you."

Heather and Dave just looked at them with confused looks. Dave asked, "Let me guess?"

"Yes, it was them."

The two men walked up to Chris and one of them said, "Are you with that beautiful woman?"

Chris didn't know what to say but he said, "Yes I am."

The other one asked, "What about the one other one?"

Chris was confused because there was only Tori. Tori came walking up to where they were standing and Chris pointed at her then said, "Do you mean her?"

Then one of the men said, "Oh heck no, we were asking about the other one."

Chris was really confused now then he remembered that Lucy was just over there talking. "Oh, you mean Lucy. Oh no, she's single and she right out there on the dance floor."

The two guys looked at each other then one of them said, "I told you that one day we would meet our special woman." Then they walked on the dance floor to talk to Lucy.

Chris went to the bar and bought a round. Then he noticed that Lisa wasn't drinking. He asked Lisa, "Do you want something to drink?

"No, I'm good and I'm driving."

He bought the round and then he did a toast. "This is to great friends and a lifetime of happiness." Then he stopped and said, "Screw that, this is to family and a lifetime of happiness." Everyone drank to that.

Tori looked at Chris and said, "Since you bought me a drink does this mean that this is a date?"

Everyone looked at him to see what he was going to say. "According to the one woman that I cuddled with, friends can buy friends drinks and stuff."

"Shut up and kiss me." Then he looked at her with a confused look and they were starting to move in for a kiss.

Before they could kiss, Lisa yelled, "I'M PREGNANT!"

Then Chris immediately turned around and yelled, "WHAT?" Tori looked at him, rolled her eyes and shook her head. Then they all congratulated Gary and Lisa. They all gave hugs, kisses or handshakes to them.

Dave said, "Oh yeah, so what about the cuddling business?"

Heather replied, "What about it?"

Dave said, "Gary and I were talking, and thought it would be nice if you guys kept doing it with us."

Heather, Lisa and Tori all looked at each other and smiled. Heather said, "We're not going nowhere." Then Heather hugged and kissed Dave. Lisa hugged and kissed Gary. Then Tori grabbed Chris, pulled him over to her and they kissed. To be continued?

The End

CUDDLES

Robert Wilt would like to thank everyone of you that took time to read his book. He hopes that you enjoyed *Cuddles* and that it kept you entertained while reading.

The Author is a factory worker that had an idea and decided to write this book. Never written a book before, Robert pursued his dream of becoming a writer which became an exciting and fun-filled journey for him. He is a lifelong resident of Monroe, Michigan and enjoys spending time with his daughter and two grandchildren. The author is also an avid sports fan who likes to bowl with his friends.

Robert Scott Wilt has an Associates Degree in Business Management, along with a certification in renewable energy.

www.ingramcontent.com/pod-product-compliance
Lightning Source LLC
Chambersburg PA
CBHW030109260626
47156CB00008B/2587

* 9 7 8 1 9 4 6 7 4 6 6 6 5 *